Christmas
POLAR BEAR

THE HOLIDAY SHIFTER MATES
BOOK TWO

KESTRA PINGREE

D1113995

Living in Fantasy

Christmas Polar Bear

Text copyright © 2018 Kestra Pingree

kestrapingree.com

All rights reserved.

No part of this book may be used or reproduced in any manner whatsoever without written permission from the author except in the case of brief quotations embodied in critical articles or reviews. Any unauthorized reproduction or distribution of this copyrighted work is illegal.

This book is a work of fiction.

August 2019 edition

First digital publication: November 2018

First print publication: December 2018

Cover design by Kestra Pingree

Printed in the U.S.A.

ISBN: 9781078738859

10 9 8 7 6 5 4 3 2

CHAPTER 1

ALMOST ANYWHERE ELSE IN the world, the Sun would have been up by now. There was a lot of dark, a lot of snow, and a lot of nothing in most of Alaska. Cedar Mongoyak was not a fan. She had reasons for leaving all of this behind. But she had also made the decision to join Trinity at the age of twenty-one, and Trinity wanted her back in Alaska at age twenty-eight.

Her stomach was full thanks to breakfast, but it wasn't settled. She sat tall with her hands resting on her plentiful thighs as she stared out the tinted window of the black SUV she was riding in, resisting the urge to smash her face against the glass like she might have done as a kid had her parents owned a vehicle. She was over the nothingness, though. She liked living in big cities, thank you. And here she was back in *Alaska* of all places.

The trees passed by as dark blotches against a luminous sky. The stars were glowing sand scattered along a dark blue beach, and bits of the sky reflected in the Tanana River like a big mirror to Cedar's left. Even with the SUV's headlights, she could see the sky better now than she had in years. Big cities were not good for star viewing thanks to all the light pollution. Hey, she never said Alaska wasn't beautiful.

She supposed she should be happy Trinity was trusting her with this, with Eurio. She *was* excited about that part, because she did her homework. All the little town really needed was some direction—hopefully—and she was nothing if not a proficient organizer. She was flattered Trinity thought she was the polar-bear shifter for the job, but that didn't help her disappointment about Alaska. She'd be spending Christmas in *Eurio* with shifters she didn't know—not that she ever went home to see her family anyway.

Cedar frowned.

A big hand waved in front of her face. Her eyes widened, and she tried to melt against the seat holding her, but she was as flat against the leather as she was going to get.

"What?" she growled. She smacked the hand away when the driver made it clear he had no intention of withdrawing on his own. She pouted and looked out the window again.

"Finally, I have your attention. You wouldn't shut up before, and then I suddenly couldn't get you out of your head."

Cedar glanced over to her left at one of Trinity's peacekeepers. He returned both hands to the steering wheel, and his eyes were on the road. The tires had caught on ice more than once since they had left Fairbanks, but Bruiser hadn't cared an ounce. The tires always found traction, and he navigated just fine in the dark. That fucked-up left eye of his didn't seem to hinder him any.

He was dangerous, a former mercenary, and not someone Cedar had spent a lot of time with. Also, he was sexy. Cedar had a thing for rough men. And all that muscle. Bruiser was ripped to hell. She just had to take one look at the corded muscles in his neck, and she knew. A man like him could handle her in bed. She was a big gal, and she liked big guys—though, unlike her type, she wasn't sporting rows upon rows of muscles.

And she didn't want to be. She liked her body. These days. It would have been a lie to say it hadn't made her self-conscious at times, but those times were no more.

"I have a lot on my mind," Cedar said quietly. She went back to staring out her window. As sexy as Bruiser was, she probably didn't want to get mixed up in *that*.

"As long as whatever's on your mind doesn't get in the way of your job, it's fine."

The ex-mercenary turned off the paved asphalt to take a hidden road within the trees. There was a lot of snow. It crunched underneath the tires, and Cedar bounced in her seat in time with the bumpy ride. She gripped the oh-shit handle to save her insides from jiggling around too much. Then she squinted her eyes at the bands of light cast by the SUV's headlights. If not for the almost-covered tire tracks of a previous vehicle coming through here, she would have missed the turn entirely. She probably would have missed it anyway. Eurio was the same kind of middle-of-nowhere town as the place she grew up in farther north.

For a while, nothing changed. Then Cedar's excellent night vision alerted her to the presence of cabins almost completely concealed within the predominantly black and white spruces.

They continued driving, and Cedar kept track of each cabin they passed. There were decent amounts of land in between most of them, leaving the town extremely spread out. She wondered if the shifters living here liked having so much space or if this added to Eurio's dysfunction. Her clan had been close together. This kind of distance would have caused problems. It would have made them strangers. She sighed, realizing she likely had her work cut out for her.

Eventually, Bruiser drove them to a clearing and onto a wide riverbank. A little wooden building that looked like a fishing shanty sat on the edge of the icy water next to a jetty.

"We're here," Bruiser said.

Sighing, Cedar mentally prepared her stiff legs for walking as she reached for the door handle. Before her fingers could meet the smooth metal, her door swung open on its own. She let out a startled squeak that would have made a chipmunk proud and a polar bear, like herself, blush in embarrassment.

"What's all this?" the culprit for her near heart attack asked. Cedar smelled bear and saw medium brown eyes glinting with the first rays of Sunlight peeking through snow-leaden branches. The stranger in front of her rivaled Bruiser in size. That was to say, she was now sitting between two hulking giants, typical bear shifter males. Unlike Bruiser, not a single scar marred the newcomer's even skin—and he was a polar bear rather than a grizzly. It was different seeing him in person. She hadn't realized how close his brown skin tone was to her own based on the pictures she had seen before coming out here; they had the same warm undertone.

"Ling couldn't make it," Bruiser replied easily.

"You're Trinity Shifters?"

"Yep. Nice to meet you, Gale." Bruiser pulled out his Trinity Peacekeeper ID anyone associated with the alliance would recognize. He reached an arm over Cedar and made sure the other shifter—Gale—could get a good look at it.

Gale grunted as he opened Cedar's door wider. "Welcome to Eurio." He held out his gloved hand, and Cedar didn't hesitate to take it. His grip was firm as his big hand engulfed hers. But, at the same time, his touch was somehow soft. He let go once she was out of the SUV. She wouldn't have minded his touch a bit longer, but this was for the best. He was also someone she probably shouldn't get involved with. So, she did her best to ignore the heat flooding her body and went to the back of the SUV to retrieve her things from the trunk.

"So, what are your names and what are you doing here?" Gale asked as Bruiser exited the SUV.

"Name's Bruiser."

Cedar glanced at the burly men as they joined her at the back of the SUV. She refitted her coat and pulled out her suitcase. She didn't pull it all the way out of the trunk, though. Gale's narrow-eyed stare made her pause.

"I'm Cedar Mongoyak," she said before Bruiser could introduce her himself. "I'll be staying in Eurio for a while to get this place in shape at Trinity's request."

Gale chuckled, but it wasn't a friendly sound. His eyes hollowed, more bear than man. "Is that right?"

"That's right," Bruiser said. "You haven't been straight with us. You've got a human resident now, and you didn't think to pass that information along?"

"We're not Trinity."

"No, but you're *allied* with Trinity to keep Eurio safe."

"We're allied with Trinity so shifters that need help can be referred to us and sent our way. Besides, Austin isn't a threat."

"All I know is Eurio doesn't keep us updated and that *might* have to do with organization." Bruiser gave

Gale a hard look with his good eye as if daring him to confess more.

Gale said nothing.

"Unless you're keeping us out of the loop on purpose."

"Wouldn't dream of it."

Bruiser sighed.

"If you're that worried about it, why not launch a full-scale interrogation? Turn Eurio inside out. Trinity has the power to do that."

Cedar stepped in. "No reason to start a fight, boys. Trinity just wants to make sure Eurio is in top shape. I'm here to assist you with whatever you might need. I'm also here to digitize your paperwork and make sure everything is up to date. No offense, but your record-keeping is atrocious."

Gale raised an eyebrow.

"I was briefed on everything Trinity knows about Eurio."

Bruiser said, "I'm just here to drop her off and make sure she's in good company."

Gale huffed out a hot breath that made white bloom in front of his face like a furious steam engine.

"But I don't know why Trinity gave me an escort," Cedar felt the need to clarify. "I'm plenty capable of taking care of myself." Not that she minded bear-shifter eye candy. Right now, she had double. God, she was warned about Gale's "uncooperative" attitude, but no one prepared her for what he was doing to her body. Once again, the pictures didn't do him justice. That heat that spread through her body had her involuntarily clenching her thighs. She wouldn't be able to hide the scent that came with her arousal.

Gale glanced at her with fire in his eyes; she was probably busted. Bruiser didn't seem to notice, though—not that she would have minded being crushed in between these two. Apparently, it had been much too long since she had been with a man. That thought dredged up a memory better left buried. Not everyone appreciated her curves, and she was used to that, but she would never be shamed for them again.

"I need to check out the human you have living here before I go," Bruiser informed.

Gale growled.

"Look, Gale. It's not a big deal. Humans and shifters together is what Trinity wants. Peaceful relations. Coexisting without having to hide what we are. Trinity wants to reveal shifters to all humans in a way that won't start some kind of shifter-human war. Because that could happen."

"I know all of that."

"Then you know how important this is."

"Yes."

Bruiser folded his arms, and Cedar tried not to drool and stare at his bulging muscles. The biceps on that guy. How? She could see them through the coat he was wearing over his standard peacekeeper combat gear. Male bear shifters really had the best bodies. Hands down.

"I don't know why Trinity is wasting their time and manpower," Gale said. "I've got everything here under control."

"All the same, I want to meet Austin Cheshire," Bruiser said. "And Cedar is staying here."

Gale pursed his lips. "Fine. School just started, but I'll take you to him." He turned on his heel, but Bruiser closed the distance between them and gripped his shoulder. Gale's entire body went rigid.

"Good. And, Gale, in the future, don't hide things. You could get Ling in trouble by asking her to keep secrets for you. Secrets don't serve anyone here. We can't build trust on them."

Gale jerked his shoulder out of Bruiser's grasp and rounded on him. Cedar thought he might take a swing at him, but his fists were clenched at his sides when he faced the peacekeeper. "Understood," he said through gritted teeth.

"I know you hate Trinity for what happened to Iris, but—"

"Not another word, Bruiser. Not if you know what's good for you. Do you want your right eye to match your left?"

The air dropped several degrees. Cedar shivered uncontrollably and gripped her arms as she hugged herself. There was way too much testosterone here. Hell, and she was squeezing her thighs together so tightly it almost hurt. She was wet, wet, wet.

"Cedar!" Bruiser roared. "Focus. You're making this difficult." His nostrils flared.

Okay, so Mr. Ex-Mercenary was aware of her needy scent too. Humans wouldn't have been able to tell she was aroused right now. She missed working with them already. That was what Trinity had her doing before: human relations. As in, she was working alongside them. None of them knew she was a shifter, but Trinity was getting closer and closer to changing that.

"Take me to Austin, and then I'm out," Bruiser said. Cedar was impressed he didn't rise to Gale's bait and turn this into a fist fight. That was also sexy. She liked the whole "be the bigger man" thing.

Cedar saluted, Bruiser rolled his eyes, and Gale didn't bother giving her a second glance.

"Might as well keep your things in the trunk," Gale said. "It'll be quicker to drive to the school."

Cedar shrugged, and then she scrambled back into her seat. She was riding shotgun because there was no way she was going to give that up for grumpy Gale. Gale quietly took a seat in the back, Bruiser started the SUV, and they moved. It was silent beyond the hum of the engine.

But not for Cedar. She found herself wondering what it would be like to sleep with a bear shifter instead of a human. She never had. It had always been men for her, humans much weaker than her. The thought of being dominated by either of the two bears with her got her heart beating a little faster. But she had a job to do. And she was no stranger to finding comfort in her fantasies. None of it would become a reality. Bruiser was leaving. Gale was off limits. She needed to focus. Besides, she wasn't really mate material anyway. That was why she had never slept with a shifter. All the polar bears she knew back home were crazy about mates and cubs, and she wasn't interested in those.

Females back home were mothers and caregivers.

When Cedar left, she learned women could be whatever they wanted to be. And she liked that freedom. She liked it a lot.

CHAPTER 2

BRUISER WASN'T INTERESTED IN driving straight to the school. He didn't even ask Gale for directions at first. He drove around aimlessly, taking Eurio in. He did his best to get Gale to talk about Eurio instead, gleaning whatever information he could while he was at it. Or maybe it was for Cedar's sake. Gale didn't know, and he didn't care. He just needed to get them out of his hair. That meant compliance. He acknowledged that Eurio's record-keeping was subpar, but he emphasized that it wasn't intentional, which was true.

It hadn't always been this way. Iris had instigated this alliance and made sure communication between

Eurio and Trinity was up to Trinity standards—but she didn't stay in a leadership position for long. She always intended on leaving what she built to Gale because she knew he would take the responsibility. She never policed him on how he did it. And she never would. She wasn't here anymore.

A part of him loathed Trinity.

Gale resisted the urge to rub his already tired eyes. He didn't need to encourage the bloodshot look he wore on almost a daily basis. It went along with that hollow feeling in his chest, an empty cavity void of even his heart. His senses were so dull he had almost missed the intensity of that she-bear's arousal.

When the SUV had gone silent again, he glanced at Cedar Mongoyak in the passenger seat and then at Bruiser in the driver's seat. Gale had the back leather bench all to himself. Had he been alone, he would have been tempted to stretch out and go back to sleep for the rest of the day. He could even get away with it sometimes since he wasn't the only Alpha in charge of Eurio. Thank the spirits for Weston.

Cedar caught his eye in the rearview mirror when he glanced in her direction again. Her eyes were brown, darker than his. Her hair was straight and silky black while his was wavy and brown, but her skin tone was nearly a perfect match to his. He was willing to bet she had ancestors from this area; the remote polar bear clans in Alaska had more in common than their life-style. It was the subtleties in her features, face in particular, nose, eyes, mouth, genes untouched by an-other race. There was also her last name. Then again, it was entirely possible she was from somewhere else. It was just an observation, a feeling he got.

And she still smelled like arousal, now that he was tuned into that fresh scent of hers. She almost didn't have a smell. It was subtle like newly fallen snow. It quietly asked him to pay attention. But he didn't want to pay attention. Sex held no appeal since Iris died.

He looked away.

"All right. Enough stalling. Tell me how to get to the school," Bruiser said.

Gale grunted. Bruiser had unzipped his coat, and Gale glimpsed the standard peacekeeper gear he wore underneath when he leaned forward to better see out the windshield. Gale focused on giving directions like the peacekeeper asked, but Ling was on the back of his mind. She was a peacekeeper too, but he trusted her. She would have told him about Cedar and Bruiser if she had been aware they were coming. He didn't like Trin-ity in Eurio's business any more than necessary. Ling knew and respected that.

Gale instructed Bruiser to drive through the winding dirt roads and into a small clearing where a new building was erected on the far edge near the white and black spruces. Soft, warm light cascaded from its windows, making it a welcoming beacon in the frozen world around it; it was the strongest source of light aside from the first signs of sunlight that would soon contend with it and eventually overpower it. Frost and snow concealed much of the wood used to construct the building, but it was easy to see the schoolhouse was brand new—especially since Bruiser had driven close to the decrepit cabins in Eurio that had noticeably collapsed roofs. Gale had no doubt the Trinity Shifters were logging away that bit of information too, comparing and contrasting everything.

So Eurio didn't have rows upon rows of sturdy cabins ready for new residents, but the shifters who did live here were well taken care of. Trinity prepped far in advance. Eurio acted in the moment. Gale was starting to like this surprise inspection less and less. If Cedar and Bruiser decided to give him a hard time, he'd point out Eurio was upgrading as times called for it. The school had a shiny new generator for starters.

Bruiser brought the SUV to a stop in front of the

schoolhouse. "So, this is the school?"

"Yes," Gale said. "Austin is teaching in there right now."

"And he's your only teacher."

"For academics. Most of us permanent residents never went to a normal school."

Cedar nodded.

"Still not ideal since you have different age groups," Bruiser said.

Gale replied, "Better than nothing. And better yet, Austin is a human. That's what Trinity wants, right?"

Cedar nodded again, vigorously this time. God, she was so damned animated. It was hard not to look at her.

After retrieving his key from the ignition, Bruiser kicked open his door and lumbered up to the school.

"Just barge in. Go right ahead," Gale mumbled as he reluctantly followed after the peacekeeper, Cedar on his heels.

Without bothering to announce himself, Bruiser flung open the door and did just that. Gale gritted his teeth as he passed through the mudroom and stopped in the large main room and only classroom in the school. Cedar shut the door behind them as several pairs of eyes locked onto them.

The school was mainly focused in this room. Beyond it, there was one other door located to the left, which contained a little hall with a bathroom and a storage room. The students were seated at tables that could hold six rather than each of them sitting at isolated desks. All students had a tablet with a variety of textbooks, lessons, and workbooks downloaded onto it. Though everyone was on a different level, Austin was making this setup work thanks to the aid of digital teachers and headphones. Eurio had some money saved up, so that wasn't an issue. Gale didn't know much about this junk, though, so Lance Lenkov had been the one in charge of the technology and in assisting Austin with getting it all up and running.

This, at least, should have looked good to the Trinity Shifters.

"Can I help you?" Austin asked.

Bruiser took an uninvited step forward, and a growl rumbled deep within Gale's chest. Austin's freckled face went a shade paler. Gale could smell the fear on him, sour and rotten. Austin pushed his glasses up the bridge of his nose, and then he wrung his hands.

Gale silenced his growling. "It's okay, Austin. This is Bruiser, and this is Cedar. They're from Trinity. They just want to check out the place. Sorry for interrupting."

Austin shook his head over and over. "No problem, Gale."

Since walking in, Gale had made a point not to let his eyes linger on the students. He was aware of them, but he wouldn't look at them—one in particular. But a certain pair of dark gray eyes found him anyway. They were lurking, coming at him from his peripheral vision. They pulled at him like a magnet, but he resisted. He couldn't turn his head and look. He wouldn't.

"I want to ask a few questions," Bruiser said.

"Sure, sure." Austin pressed his lips together after speaking, likely to stop their trembling. Gale didn't like seeing one of his own anxious like this. At least Mateo wasn't here. A fight would be imminent.

One of the students stood and went to Austin's side. Gale didn't make direct eye contact then either, but he couldn't pretend not to see his cub now. Ike. He brushed his arm against Austin's in a sign of trust and moved just a little closer. Then Neil, a wolf shifter, got out of his chair as Bruiser took another step forward. Janice, a red-tailed hawk shifter, stood too and followed Neil to Austin's other side.

"Easy." Bruiser held up his hands in a placating

gesture. "I'm not going to hurt your teacher."

The students up front didn't budge and those in their chairs were restless. Austin let out a jittery laugh, but he was relieved. Gale could smell it, a subtle sweetness in the air. He could even taste it like a dusting of sugar on his tongue. His coiled muscles relaxed, and he folded his arms. He even chuckled. Eurio was a mess, but it was united when it mattered. "Ask your questions, Bruiser."

"Why'd you come here?" the peacekeeper asked.

"I came for Mateo." Austin's voice was suddenly clear. "He's my mate."

"And a wolf shifter," Gale added in case Bruiser didn't know that part. Gale didn't know what Trinity told him before coming here.

"I know about Mateo Diaz," Bruiser said.

Gale wanted to growl again, but he didn't. He didn't like Bruiser. It wasn't just his Trinity Shifter or peacekeeper status. Gale didn't like the crushing weight of his presence. He knew peacekeepers were powerful. Iris had been one of the best, and she was more of an alpha than Gale would ever be, but it didn't mean he had to like it. He had a hunch Bruiser was concentrating his dominance on him specifically, though. Did he consider Gale a threat?

"You don't mind shifters then," Bruiser continued. "And you're willing to keep our secret because you know it'd be disastrous for your mate, at the very least, if you didn't."

"I knew Mateo wasn't human back in high school. I didn't see him for four years after I figured that out, and I still didn't tell anyone about him," Austin said. "I never will. Hunters almost killed me and Mateo." His hand went to the space between his neck and left shoulder. He rubbed his fingers against the bite that had scarred over, the mark and consequential scent that made him undeniably Mateo's. "I'm not stupid. I can imagine how people might react to a sudden wide-scale discovery of shifters. Gale said Trinity wants to out shifters slowly and ease humans into it."

"Gale is correct. We want peaceful relations. More and more shifters live among unaware humans every day. Trinity is promoting that. If humans have already been working peacefully alongside shifters for years, it should smooth things out once they know what we are. We'll have advocates, humans who are friends with shifters—or even mates. But we need to do this delicately. The scale could easily tip one way or another, in our favor or not, depending on how things are handled."

"I agree," Austin said.

"Looks like there's no problem here, Bruiser." Cedar raised her hand and wiggled her plump fingers at him. "You can go now."

"I used to hate humans," Neil said, puffing out his chest as he stood in front of Austin. He was ten, shorter than his teacher, but growing taller every day. He, like most of the kids his age, was on a growth spurt.

"But not this one, huh?" Cedar asked with a smile. Gale was caught off-guard. Her smile was warm, genuine. Her eyes twinkled, sparkling gold in the warm light of the school.

The wolf shifter nuzzled Austin's arm. "He's nice. He likes us. He doesn't call us mangy garbage diggers and chase us out of town." Neil was from a small naturalist pack of wolf shifters who had tried to avoid humans, but when times got hard, they were reduced to digging in human garbage for food. Gale was glad Weston had found them.

Austin laughed as the kid nuzzled his arm again, but he didn't seem bothered by the primal gesture of affection. Mateo had a good mate, and Gale was happy for him. Both of them. Even when it made the hollow ache in his chest grow.

Bruiser nodded in what Gale hoped was approval.

Cedar grinned wider. Gale wasn't sure he had ever seen a sunnier face. It was like her skin was emitting sunrays. His eyes lingered on the distinct dimple on the right side of her mouth before he could tear them away.

Suddenly bold, Austin stepped forward and held out his hand. The students obediently stayed where they were. Bruiser took his hand and shook. "Good to meet you, Austin Cheshire."

"Good to meet you too, Bruiser."

"This setup is crude, though," Cedar said.

"Have you seen the tablets?" Gale defended. "Technology of any sort is a big step up for this town."

"I can see that."

"And Austin does an excellent job."

The rest of the students stood up. As if to back up Gale's statement, they clustered together at their teacher's side.

"I can see that too," Cedar said. She folded her arms and tapped her skin playfully. She looked so soft. Not a peacekeeper. "Eurio isn't a lost cause."

"Grab your things, Cedar," Bruiser said. "Then I'll get going. Unless you want me to drop you off somewhere first?"

"We mostly walk around here," Gale said. "You can go."

"Yeah, I haven't seen many cars." Cedar shrugged. "Meet me outside, Gale." She beamed at the class. "Thank you for your time, everyone! It was lovely meeting you." She daintily waved her hand and turned around with an exaggerated sway of her hips. Gale's eyes went straight to her plentiful ass. It was framed perfectly in the black form-fitting pants she wore; it was hard not to look. He managed to tear his eyes away, but dark gray caught in his peripheral vision yet again.

His cub was looking at him, begging him to look back. Gale turned. He tried to answer Ike's silent plea, but he couldn't meet his stormy eyes. He focused instead on the dark brown of his hair. It was shaved on the sides of his head, but the top was long enough to be pulled into a ponytail. It was how all male cubs wore their hair in the Loike Clan. Gale had worn his the same way.

Ike's lips quirked, revealing the barest hint of white teeth. Gale's chest ached, dull and somehow pronounced.

Sometimes, he could smile back. Today wasn't one of those times.

He turned his back on his cub and left, bearing all of his shame in silence.

CHAPTER 3

IT WAS QUIET IN Eurio, the kind of quiet Cedar wasn't accustomed to. In the big cities, quiet was never quiet. There was the sound of cars rushing by her apartment window, the buzz of street lamps, and voices of passersby on the sidewalks below. Now it was her and Gale with nothing but the dull crunch of snow underfoot.

She was starting to miss Bruiser. He wasn't a conversationalist exactly, but he was warm and friendly compared to Gale. Gale was cold as ice, and yet her body insisted he was as hot as a wildfire. She had gotten a hold of herself when they set out in silence together—more or less. Then she fell behind and got the perfect view of his ass, and she had to remind herself to stay cool. He was just in jeans, but damn did his ass look fine.

Bruiser was right. She needed to focus. She was on a job. She was here to make sure Gale wasn't hiding anything else important from Trinity. Bringing Austin here without consulting the shifter alliance was a red flag.

Cedar sighed and considered Iris. It was no secret Gale blamed Trinity for the loss of his mate. She was a peacekeeper on Trinity business after all, so that wasn't surprising. But did it mean Gale wasn't fit for his position in Eurio? She had no idea what his mental state was like. Then again, she was no psychologist. However, she hadn't missed the way Gale had blatantly ignored his cub back at the school. Isaac kept trying to catch his father's eye, and Gale wouldn't have it.

Why did Trinity insist *she* keep an eye on Gale during her time here? The guy needed a counselor or something. This was not her area of expertise.

Cedar looked down at Gale's footprints. She took her next step carefully, making sure not to make new prints of her own. Following him like that was like being a cub again. Her feet were much smaller than his, so it wasn't difficult to merge their trails into one; the hardest part was matching his long-legged stride. Doing that fought off the silence for a little while, but it didn't work for long.

White spruces. Black spruces. The occasional cabin here and there. This place was bleak, and there weren't any Christmas lights to help it out. There weren't any decorations at all.

Cedar couldn't take the nearly deafening silence anymore. "So where will I be staying?" she asked and shifted her handbag to keep it from digging into her shoulder. "You didn't say. You just took my suitcase and started walking, and I grabbed the rest of my things, and I started following because 'we mostly walk around here,' and Bruiser left."

"You didn't bring much," Gale said without looking back. "It's light." His voice was almost lost in the wind.

"I don't own much. Are you going to answer my question?"

"I didn't know you'd be coming or staying, so I didn't prepare a place beforehand."

Cedar had figured out that much. She rolled her eyes behind him. It was a harmless action. It wasn't like he could see it—unless he had eyes hidden in the back of his head. He could have. His light brown hair was thick and fell in waves down the back of his neck. Shaggy, shaggy, shaggy. He had to be due for a haircut. Cedar thought it would be cute if he shaved the sides and styled his hair like his son's. It was a good look on the boy, and she was certain it would suit the father. Isaac was young, and his face had that youthful roundness to it, but he was well on his way to growing into a mini Gale—aside from the features he must have gotten from his mother: stormy gray eyes and dark brown hair.

Gale continued, "Your options are limited. You'll either need to stay with someone or brave a leaky cabin."

She was *not* going to "brave a leaky cabin." She saw those things for herself when Bruiser was driving them around aimlessly in the SUV. They needed to be condemned.

"So I'll stay with you," she said. It made the most sense. Gale should have all the records she needed, or whatever paperwork this place kept, and then she'd get to decide if he could handle being an Alpha here with all his extra emotional baggage. God, that sounded like a big deal when she actually thought about it. *This is all you. No pressure or anything, Cedar,* she mused.

"I have a better idea," Gale said. "You'll want an internet connection and cell reception to keep in touch with Trinity without having to go to Fairbanks periodically, right?"

Appalled, Cedar asked, "You don't even have landline phones that work? I swear you do."

"One, and it's public. You want to make your Trinity business public?"

Cedar shrugged, but the gesture was lost on Gale. He hadn't looked back at her once. It was like talking to a mountain. "You've recently started fixing all that though, haven't you? I saw the school."

"Yeah, but it's slow going, and plenty of shifters still want a section of the town without. You know we have residents who have torn out their generators to leave their homes without electricity, don't you? I'm sure that was in your briefing."

"Yes." Cedar huffed. "Have these shifters ever seen Christmas lights? Maybe that would change their minds."

"This place decorates itself. An aurora is much more beautiful than Christmas lights could ever be."

"Sure, but what about when there isn't an aurora? Christmas lights, Gale. Do you guys hate Christmas too? It's the perfect opportunity to get together, to give gifts and reach out to each other. Maybe Eurio is a little too spread out. Maybe it has a little too much space."

For a moment, the grumpy polar bear was quiet. He puffed out even breaths of hot air that were punctuated by their visibility in the cold. And the sound. Cedar liked the sound of his breathing. She hadn't noticed it before above the crunching snow. It was quiet, a warm sound that wrapped around her chest like a blanket.

"Anyway," Gale said gruffly. "As I was saying, we have one cabin that pretty much has everything you could need—though he likes to be stingy about it."

"Gale, Christmas lights."

"You can go to Fairbanks if you want an electric light show, Cedar. I'll let you drive one of our few SUVs. I'll even let you keep it."

"Trying to get rid of me already," she grumbled.

If Gale heard that remark, he decided not to comment. And everything went silent again. The Sun overhead felt like Cedar's only companion. Gale was nothing more than the shadows cast by the trees.

"How much longer until we get to this 'stingy' guy?" Cedar asked. She was fed up with this whole scenario. Then she heard the distinct buzz of a generator close by.

"We're here," Gale said.

Within the trees sat another cabin. Surprise, surprise. It didn't look like anything special—aside from the big-ass generator attached to its side. That thing was working hard. The snow around it didn't stand a chance with the heat it was producing. That seemed a little dangerous, like a possible fire hazard.

Gale marched right up to the front door, dropped Cedar's suitcase on the porch, and opened the door without so much as a knock. *He and Bruiser really need to work on their manners,* Cedar thought irritably as she followed her escort inside, shutting the door behind her like a civilized shifter.

"Uh. What the fuck, Gale?" said a male, but Cedar didn't see him. She was too busy gasping, startled by the sudden blast of heat. She was going to melt in here. This cabin was a furnace just like its generator outside. There was a mountain of medical texts and various computer bits everywhere, leaving only specks of wooden floorboards to shine through the mess.

Finally, she spotted the shifter who spoke. He was sitting snug in the center of chaos on a cleared patch of floor, and he was wearing nothing more than his boxers. But she couldn't care less about that. She was seeking a lifeline, and her eyes were drawn to a nearby window. She stumbled through junk to get to it and opened it without asking. The cold air clawed through the palpable heat, and Cedar sucked in a breath, clearing her lungs. She had nearly felt like she was suffocating. If she was going to be in here for long, she was probably going to strip too.

"You should be thanking us for saving your life," Gale said, giving the guy on the floor a pointed look. "Why is it so goddamn hot in here, Lance?"

"I hadn't noticed."

"No? You're sweating."

This shifter smelled feline. And his skin was the whitest Cedar had ever seen in her life; with all that sweat dripping down his body, it looked like melting porcelain. His paleness was especially noticeable because of the dark inky lines of his almost endless tattoos. She realized she recognized him now that she could think. He was a Lenkov, one of the tiger shifter twins. She had been briefed on them too.

Lance sighed. "What do you want?"

"You still got that extra room?" Gale asked.

The tiger shifter's eyes narrowed. They were a pale blue at first, but when the light hit them just right, they turned red. "Extra room?"

"Last I checked, you and Yuri share a room."

"That's none of your damn business."

"And yet it's not hard to figure out. The room you share is the only place in the cabin that isn't trashed. The bed isn't even visible in your extra room. You couldn't sleep in there."

"And you think I'm going to clean it out?"

"Yeah, because I need it."

"For her? Fuck you."

It was time to intervene. "Hi, I'm Cedar." She held up her hand and fluttered her fingers. "Also, I didn't agree to this arrangement."

"Yeah. No, Gale," Lance said, folding his arms around his middle. Goosebumps pocked his skin as another frigid breeze forced its way inside of the room. Cedar closed the window halfway, hoping that would regulate the temperature well enough to suit the two polar bears and the Siberian tiger who had acclimated himself to deathly heat levels.

"Why not?"

Lance growled. "*You're* the one with a spare, *empty* room since Mateo moved out into his own cabin with Austin. Use it instead of trying to pawn this lady off on me and Yuri. And, if you haven't noticed, I'm still in my boxers. Could you leave and shut the door now?" He flippantly waved his hand. "Next time it'll be locked."

"Where is Yuri?" Gale asked. He folded his big arms in an I-mean-business stance.

"He's sleeping." Lance averted his gaze, returning his reddish-blue eyes to his computer screen. It was filled with lines of text. What was this guy doing? Researching something? Based on the book titles scattered about the room, he was fascinated by the brain. It had to be because of his brother.

"I haven't seen him out all week," Gale said.

Lance didn't move his eyes away from the screen. "He's not feeling well."

"So why won't you let anyone take a look at him?"

Lance slammed his hands against a precarious pile of books, toppling them. Then he kicked them away. Loose papers danced in the air and some caught in the wind, escaping out the window. His shoulders rolled forward as he lumbered toward Gale. He stayed hunched over until he reached him and stood up tall to face him. He was barely shorter than the polar bear, but Gale had him beat in terms of muscle mass. Still, Lance held his ground.

"I don't know what you're trying to do, Gale, if you really think I'm going to let that chick stay here with us or if you're making an excuse to come inside and check on us, but *get out*."

Their blazing eyes locked, neither one of them blinking. Cedar's breath caught, as if in sync with their stares. The whirring machines grew silent. Even time seemed to stop.

"I thought we learned to trust each other by now." Gale's voice was a low rumble that made time move once again, like pressing play on a remote. "I care about Yuri too, Lance. We all do. If he's getting worse again, I need to know. Maybe you made your decision before based on my own reaction to the idea, but we could still ask for a—"

"Get *out!*" Lance shouted.

"It's *his* life! Let him make the final decision. At least run it by him."

Cedar was about to jump in as a peacemaker when a door screeched open. The other Lenkov emerged from a dark hall, rubbing the bruised skin underneath his tired light brown eyes. In some ways, he looked a lot like Lance: the straight cut of his nose, his lean musculature, the tattoos adorning his shirtless chest (at least he was wearing pants). In other ways, he looked completely different, mainly in their distinct color palettes. Yuri was painted with warm colors while Lance was painted with cool colors.

"What's going on out here?" Yuri asked and

rubbed his eyes again. "It's loud." He looked at Gale. Then he looked at Lance.

Lance held up his hands and signed something. Cedar had no idea what. She didn't know much about American Sign Language.

And Gale signed something, but he spoke too. "How are you doing? I came to check on you, but your brother tried to kick me out."

Yuri glanced at Lance again. His face was impassive, a blank stone slate; it didn't help that Cedar couldn't see his mouth clearly through his beard. "I'm fine," he said. "Who's the she-bear?"

"Cedar," Gale signed what had to be her name. "She's from Trinity. She'll be staying in Eurio for a while."

Cedar waved again. She decided against saying anything since Yuri wouldn't have been able to make sense of her words anyway. She had never heard of Pure Word Deafness before, but it was apparently a thing. Yuri could hear and understand everything just fine except for spoken words. It was caused by a seizure he had had when he was sixteen. It messed up part of his brain. Luckily, the Lenkovs had been living in Eurio around two years by that point.

Iris, Gale, and Ling found the tiger twins when

they were fourteen. They were the starting point of Eurio's transformation into a shifter haven. The Pure Word Deafness was likely the reason the twins hadn't moved on from this place. It had been ten years now. Cedar doubted they had any intention of ever leaving. Yuri's seizures were getting worse, based on this back-and-forth verbal aggression between Gale and Lance. Trinity hadn't known that. Therefore, Cedar hadn't known that. This was one of the reasons why Eurio needed to step up on its reports. This was why Cedar had to evaluate Gale. Trinity couldn't help if they didn't have proper records and if they weren't continually informed on current situations.

Yuri smelled sick. Close-to-death sick.

"Hi, Cedar," Yuri said. "Everything's fine here. Sorry if Lance freaked you out."

Lance signed something with rapid-fire motions. Yuri signed back just as quickly. And Gale joined in. Cedar was left looking every which way. All she could get out of the furious movements and facial expressions was discontent. Gale was exasperated. He puffed out a breath and shook his head.

"I'm okay," Yuri insisted, dropping his hands to his sides. "Just a cold. It'll go away soon. And I'm going back to bed, so see you guys later. Be nice, Lance." He turned tail and disappeared somewhere inside of the dark hall.

"You two better not be lying," Gale said.

"Even if we were, what could you do about it?" Lance taunted.

Cedar held up her hands. "Okay, boys. That's quite enough. Don't you think? Lance, Gale and I will leave you and your brother to it. But if you need anything, you let us know, all right?"

Lance scoffed, "Whatever, lady. I don't even know you."

"We'll have to fix that then." She held out her hand to him. "I'm Cedar Mongoyak, and I'm here to help get Eurio in order."

"Order?" Lance laughed.

"Yep." She wiggled her hand.

Lance rolled his eyes, but he moved close enough to her to take her hand when he extended his own. He gave her hand one firm shake before letting go. "Have fun with that."

Cedar nodded. "Okay, Gale. Let's get going."

"Got yourself a new boss bear, Gale? She's been here a whole two seconds and she's already whipped you into submission," Lance goaded.

Cedar said nothing, and Gale didn't take the bait—

though his shoulders visibly stiffened. He opened the door and gestured for Cedar to go first. She did, and he followed without incident, shutting the door behind him.

"You handled him pretty well." Gale reclaimed Cedar's suitcase and took the lead, trampling untouched snow as he set off in a new direction.

"Is he always so abrasive?" Cedar asked.

"Pretty much."

"You're worried about them."

Gale said nothing. He just walked on with those broad shoulders pulled back to accentuate all of his intimidating might. God, and his firm ass. Cedar had another lovely view of that. She didn't mind walking behind him for that reason alone. She squeezed her thighs together in a sorry attempt to ask her body to behave. Why did he have to be her physical type? She had a million other much more pressing things to think about.

She sighed. "This place is a real disaster, isn't it? I've got my work cut out for me."

"Welcome to Eurio."

CHAPTER 4

"YOU'LL BE STAYING HERE," Gale said. "It's not much, and I don't have a reliable internet connection."

"You have electricity, so I'll still be able to use my laptop," Cedar replied.

Gale shrugged. "Perfect then."

"I'm hoping you keep some records here too. Paperwork at the very least?"

"Some."

"Does Weston have 'some' too?"

"Yep, a little bit here and there. Whatever's important."

"Spirits," Cedar mumbled. She dropped her medium-sized bag next to her suitcase at the foot of what used to be Mateo's bed and ran her hand over the crude wooden frame. Eurio didn't bother with refined looks. It went for functionality first. She left her hand there, her touch soft to avoid any splinters.

"Spirits," Gale repeated. "Mongoyak. Are you originally from around here, Cedar?"

"Farther north. I used to be part of the Ruet Clan. They live much more secluded than you do in Eurio, though. There's also much more time spent as a polar bear."

She pulled her laptop out of her bag and moved over to the small desk and chair; aside from the bed, they were the only things that had previously occupied the abandoned room. Her thighs spilled off the edges of the chair when she sat down, and she took a moment to make sure she was centered. She kicked off her boots and crossed her little feet. Then she opened her laptop, booting it up as she drummed her fingers against rough wood.

Gale kept catching whiffs of her potent scent. Sometimes it had an undeniably sweet quality. Like now. It was constant arousal. She either found him extremely attractive, or her bear was ready to mate. It would have been out of season for mating, so he supposed it was the former. The polar-bear shifters in or from clans usually preferred a single life partner rather than finding a suitable match for seasonal breeding anyway—not that any of this speculation made her scent easier to deal with.

"Get me those records," she said. "Whatever you have. Files on the shifters living here, information about the town, a map, literally everything."

He hadn't realized she was looking over her shoulder at him. Had he been staring? He was suddenly self-conscious and cast his gaze to the wall to avoid eye contact. "Sure," he said.

He went to his room and opened the closet. At the foot of it sat a bunch of dusty boxes. It had been a while since he looked at these files or added to them. Most of the information Trinity got from Eurio these days was word of mouth, Gale to Ling to Trinity. He wondered if any of this junk was relevant. But that wasn't his problem. It was Cedar's. He piled up the boxes and took them back to her room without bothering to inspect their contents. Cedar's eyes widened as he dropped the dusty boxes in one tall pile on the floor next to her desk.

"You know, Trinity should already have all of this information," he said.

"Yeah, well, I have to fact check and update them on everything I can. Trinity wants to make sure Eurio is the best it can be. Costs and expenses...," Cedar muttered. "Spreadsheets, here I come." She sighed. "I'll write up a schedule for you too."

"What kind of schedule?"

"Rehabilitation. Eurio is growing bigger because fewer shifters are leaving. Eurio is mostly meant to be a stopgap. These shifters are supposed to, essentially, be rehabilitated and sent back out into this human-dominated world. Remember? You're supposed to be helping them know how to do that."

"We don't force anyone to leave."

"No, but you don't really give them the option to either. It's easier here. It's safe."

"That's damn right. A lot of these shifters have been hurt by humans, and we're not a boot camp."

"I'm not talking about a rigorous get-up-at-five-and-do-push-ups-every-morning kind of schedule, Gale. Life skills. I'm talking about life skills out in the human world. These shifters have been hurt in the past, but they shouldn't be hiding in Eurio because they're scared of getting hurt again if they leave. Trinity doesn't want to force these shifters out of Eurio either. We just want them educated. Eurio is only so big, right?

You can't expect to keep absolutely everyone who comes your way, and I'm sure a good amount want to go out and find their place, but they have to find the courage first. They won't be alone either. Ideally, they should keep in contact with Eurio and Trinity in case they ever need help again. Eurio is a home base. It's building connections. It's all good things, Gale. What are you trying to protect Eurio from?"

Trinity, he thought. He knew it was contradictory. But that didn't change anything. It didn't change the weights and chains entrapping his heart.

"Forget it," Cedar said. "Just tell me when dinner's ready, all right? We missed lunch, and I'm hungry. Aren't you hungry? I hope missing lunch isn't a normal thing around here."

Gale chuckled. Some of the things this she-bear said felt off the wall, quirky. "Oh, I'll tell you about dinner."

Cedar scowled. "What's with that tone?"

He leaned in closer to her, his lips nearly pressed against her ear. She sucked in a breath and didn't let it go. But her face was still bright, sunny. Her pure scent sweetened again. It all stirred something in him he wanted to ignore, energy sparking in his core. It got his dick excited.

"You'll have to work for it," he whispered.

She tilted her head. Their lips could have touched if one of them moved just an inch closer. She met his gaze with a hard look of her own. Gold shone in her eyes like sunbeams. He knew that light, that energy. It was Solsis. "I can catch whatever you try to throw at me, Gale. So do your worst."

She was indomitable. And that one specific quality, the Sun Magic flickering in her eyes, reminded Gale of Iris.

He hated it.

It wasn't Cedar's fault. He could find Iris in anyone because she wouldn't leave him.

She wouldn't leave.

"We'll see, Mongoyak," Gale said, matching Cedar's intense stare. "We'll see."

Ike growled and tugged on Gale's hand, overcoming the slippery grip of their gloves. He was a handful, a rough-and-tumble kind of kid. He didn't usually bother wrestling with Gale, though. He didn't do it with anyone who wasn't willing—Gale's rules. Now that Mateo didn't live with them anymore, Ike didn't have a consistent outlet. So he tried this more often with Gale, getting his way by being physical. Since school started, Gale tried to be a model parent by taking Ike to school and picking him up; he didn't always succeed at even that. Ike knew his way around Eurio, but he was seven years old. Gale didn't like him out on his own, but sometimes getting out of bed was the hardest thing in the world. Austin had almost offered to take care of school and Ike for him. Mateo stopped him. He had even said, "You do it. He's your kid, and you don't have an excuse."

He was right. Gale didn't have a valid excuse.

"Dad, I don't want to go home! I want to go to the Hunt. Please." Ike tugged harder on his father's hand.

Gale slowed to a stop, the snow under his feet groaning in protest before being silenced. "You remember that she-bear with me when I went to your class this morning?"

The struggling stopped. Ike tried to catch his father's eye. This time Gale answered. He met his son's gaze and did his best to push thoughts of Iris aside. He let her memory niggle at him underneath the surface, but he contained it.

"Yes," Ike said.

"She's staying in Mateo's old room. We're only going home to pick her up."

"She's joining the Hunt, too?"

"Yep, if she doesn't catch anything, she doesn't get dinner." Gale learned Cedar was a polar bear and from Alaska, but it was clear she had led a pampered life for years, a mostly human life. It would be interesting to see if she had retained any of her skills. He was willing to bet her bear was out of practice.

"You're fishing with me?" Ike asked.

"Yes, I'm fishing with you." Gale lightly pulled on his cub's little ponytail.

Ike's eyes lit up and a huge grin overtook his mouth, showing white teeth and a couple gaps left by missing baby teeth. "Let's go get her! What's her name again?"

"Cedar."

"Let's get Cedar!" Now Ike was tugging Gale's hand for a different reason. They practically ran the rest of the way home.

When they barged into the house, Cedar was in the hall outside of her room. "There you are," she said. "You didn't say you were leaving, Gale."

"We're going fishing," Ike announced. He stood tall with his shoulders rolled back as he walked up to

Cedar. He tried to be still, mirroring his father's stance. But with the way he rocked back and forth on the balls of his feet, it was obvious he was trying to contain his pent-up energy. It was good to know Ike hadn't forgotten his manners, though. New shifters didn't usually like to be crowded. Personal space was the most valuable thing Eurio had to offer. "You have to if you want dinner," Ike explained.

"Is that right?" Cedar said.

"Think you can handle that, office girl?" Gale asked.

"Oh, I know how to fish. Didn't you listen to what I said earlier? I'm practically *from* here. I was expecting much more, Gale. Your bark is worse than your bite."

"And how many years has it been since you fished?"

She shrugged. "I assume we aren't talking about human fishing, you know, with a pole, line, and hook."

Ike wrinkled his nose. "No, we fish with our bare hands." He tried to hide a laugh and ended up snorting. "Our *bear* hands! That's funny, right?"

"Very funny." Gale ruffled his cub's hair, disheveling his perfect ponytail.

Cedar smirked. "Wonderful." She walked forward, bypassing Ike, and stood in front of Gale. She was about a head shorter than him, but she only tilted her head up to catch his eyes, refusing to crane her neck. She placed her hand on his covered chest and patted it. "Challenge accepted."

Her fingers burned right through the fabric.

CHAPTER 5

IF CEDAR WAS INTIMIDATED, she wasn't showing it.

"Joining the party today, Gale?" Weston asked. His smirk wrinkled the scar on his nose.

"Brought company," Gale said. "Cedar Mongoyak from Trinity."

The she-bear stepped up to exchange pleasantries with the Toran Pack Alpha, Weston, and his mate, Cary. She was unperturbed by all the pairs of eyes watching her. Most of Eurio was here. If they all hunted together, it was much more likely everyone would get dinner. This was Eurio's organization. They'd help each other, but none of this was required. Shifters could go out, hunt on their own, and hardly have any interaction with anyone else. Gale and Weston checked in occasionally to make sure everyone had what they needed, but that was the extent of Eurio's order. It worked well enough for them.

Gale scanned the crowd of shifters for the Lenkovs. But they were absent. He wasn't surprised, but it made him bristle. If he didn't see Yuri out soon, looking *much* better, he was going to do something the brothers wouldn't like.

"Old bear." Mateo came up from behind Gale and slapped his back hard enough to make him lurch. "Didn't expect to see you here." He was basically bald with that buzzed hair of his, and he wasn't wearing a hat. His cheeks and nose were tinted red because of it.

"Ike wanted me to come, and I've got a Trinity Shifter to babysit," Gale said.

"This *Trinity Shifter* changed your mind?" Mateo flicked a look to Cedar. "Ike asked you before, but you never came."

Gale scowled.

"What's with that look?"

"Trinity."

"What about it? I thought you loved it. You

worked your ass off to sell it to Austin back in Glasglow."

"I also went behind Trinity's back to make sure you didn't get yourself killed."

Mateo stopped paying attention. He was looking around for someone. Gale figured he knew who when he caught sight of Ike stalking Mateo. Bears weren't exactly known for stealth though, and Mateo was ready to catch him. But Ike knew that too, so he pushed it farther. He launched himself like a rocket, aiming straight for Mateo's chest, and succeeded in toppling the wolf shifter over. The cub growled in triumph as he pinned the twenty-one-year-old beneath him in the snow and playfully bit at his neck.

"I got you, Mateo," he said. "I got you!"

Mateo growled and snapped back. "You sure did. I forget how big you're getting."

Ike puffed out his chest, and Mateo took the opportunity to roll them over, trapping the cub underneath him now.

"Not fair," Ike complained. But he was smiling and laughing as Mateo nuzzled his cheek. Both of them were dusted in snow, but they were protected by their winter layers. Soon they would rely only on their fur coats. They were used to the cold—Austin, on the other hand, was not.

The human rubbed one arm as his other hand held a thermos containing a piping hot drink. He took a tiny sip and snuggled up against Mateo's side when he and Ike stood up. Ike leaned against Mateo too, but his eyes were trained on the icy Tanana River.

Gale caught sight of his parents out of the corner of his eye. They were coming right for him. He braced himself for whatever Mama and Papa Blanc might have to tell him, and he spoke first. "Yes, I know. I haven't shown face at the Hunt for a while."

His mother smiled, accentuating her deeply engraved laugh lines, and gave him one of the bear hugs she was so well known for. "It's good to see you, Gale."

"No pearls of wisdom?"

Papa Blanc grasped Gale's shoulder with his big hand. His grip was fierce. At fifty-one, most shifters still held their age very well, even though their lifespans weren't much different from a human's.

"Who's the she-bear?" Papa Blanc asked.

"She's a Trinity Shifter come to set Eurio straight," Gale explained.

"Papa Blanc!" Ike shouted. He ran to his grandfather, who met him with open arms. He swept the cub off his feet and high into the air.

"How's my favorite grandcub?"

"I'm your only grandcub."

Sometimes, more often than he cared to admit, Gale wondered if his parents should have been the ones raising Ike. They had taken care of him for a year after Iris died, but then they said they wouldn't do it anymore. Then, when Ike was just two years old, Gale moved him out to Glasglow, Utah, after hearing about a young wolf shifter who lost his parents to hunters. That wolf shifter was Mateo. Gale uprooted Ike at every turn, and, in some ways, it seemed like he favored Mateo over his own flesh and blood. Maybe he did to a degree. He could connect to Mateo in a way he couldn't connect to Ike.

Iris, Gale thought, *why did you have to leave us? Why'd you have to leave me? I don't know how to be a good father to our cub even though I've been trying my damnedest.*

He looked at Ike, forcing a smile when his cub gave a tentative grin. It felt like a direct punch to his heart.

"All right, everyone!" Weston shouted. "We're about to start the Hunt. Catch something for dinner tonight. That's the goal. Whoever gets the most food gets head chef. You'll delegate preparations, oversee all the dishes. Yeah, it's a lot of work, but you'll get exactly what you want. That's the trade-off. So go hard. Catch fish, rabbits, elk, whatever you can sink your teeth into. Hunt ends at sundown. Ready?"

Cedar stood beside Weston with her arms folded. She was barely holding in a grin. It was like she was trying to trap sunbeams. The light found ways to shine through her skin because it was so intense. Gale shook his head. It was all in his head. She wasn't glowing, not literally. *Eyes on the prize,* he told himself. He was going to get the most fish. Just a little friendly competition between a pampered office shifter and a shifter who lived in the wild. What right did *she* have to come and change Eurio's inner-workings?

"GOOOO!" Weston howled.

Almost every shifter who came to the Tanana River tore out of their clothes and shifted mid-run in a noisy chorus. Blurs of mostly white rushed for the river, and earth-toned blurs ran for the trees. Ike was one of the first to hit the water. Gale watched him from the riverbank. In the next couple seconds, Ike reemerged with a big silvery sheefish. He tossed it onto the shore in an empty snowy space now claimed as his catch pile. The riverbank would fill up with plenty more of those soon.

"I think the bears have an advantage," Austin

mused. "More fish in the river than game out in the trees." He took another sip of his hot drink and stared out at the water and the trampled bits of ice. "I never thought I'd be living in a nudist society located in Alaska of all places."

"The nudist part or the Alaska part?" Gale asked.

"Both."

Gale chuckled. "At least it doesn't shock you anymore." Aside from him and Austin, Cedar was the only other one still standing around. "You know this is a competition, right?" Gale asked. "What are you doing?"

"I could ask you the same thing," she said. Then she removed her coat. She took her sweet time. She either didn't give a damn about the competition or she was that confident in her skills. Gale was the latter. "Do you mind?" Cedar asked as she pulled off her sweater, leaving her topless aside from her bra. Her brown skin looked so soft. Her breasts were perfectly framed.

Gale did look away, but he didn't want to. He gazed out at the polar bears going crazy in the river. By now they had dispersed, finding their own fishing spots and fighting for upstream positions. He should probably get going if he was going to win.

When Gale glanced back at Cedar, she had entirely disrobed. Goosebumps covered her flesh, but her hair was long enough to act as a blanket—though it wasn't long enough to cover her powerful thighs and her plentiful ass. She hunched over, and the air filled with gunfire: her bones breaking and reshaping. She grew much larger as white fur sprouted all over her body. Gale fixated on the change in her face: her now black nose, the small round ears on top of her head. She was a beauty of a woman, so it should have been no surprise that her polar bear was no less stunning.

She flicked her gold-hued eyes at him and lumbered to the water. She jumped in with a big splash. Water droplets and ice shards flew, catching some of the last rays of sunlight; they shone the same shade of gold as her eyes. It was molten lava. And it stirred something in his bear.

"Better get going, Gale," Austin said.

After giving his head a good shake, Gale tore out of his winter gear in mere seconds. He called on his bear the moment his bare skin touched the frigid air. Gunfire sounded once again. Then his big paws were moving, carrying him effortlessly through the snow, and he leaped into the water. His water-repellent fur kept the cold at bay as he followed Cedar downstream since most everyone else was fighting for upstream. He just needed to find a good area that hadn't been touched or frightened away, pick it clean, and keep on the move.

The first fish he saw was a burbot. He sunk his teeth in it before it knew he was there and tossed it ashore next to the nearest tree. The base of its trunk would be his stash. Then he saw a northern pike. He scooped that one up just as quickly, biting down and stopping its wiggling before tossing it onto his pile. He had laser-point focus and quickly made up for lost time. Fish after fish, he tossed them onto his pile. When he had cleared out this section of the river, he moved on. He used the current to assist him in his speedy pursuit of fleeing fish. He had just caught a huge sheefish and was about to return to his stash when he spotted Cedar's. She had at least five more fish than he did. *Five.* And he was going at a record speed!

He did his best to ignore her. He still had time. Where was the next fish? They had become scarce, wise to the fact they were being hunted. Then he saw one, the biggest sheefish yet. Its silver scales reflected the light and gave it away just in time; the sun was all but gone from the sky. He pushed off the rocks of the river bed and zoomed through the water. The fish was in his grasp, his big paws and claws ready for the kill, but then the water went white with millions of bubbles. A big white paw stole the fish from him in one graceful swoop. However, by then it was too late to stop his forward momentum. He collided with the other polar bear, and they grappled for the fish. They emerged from the river with roars. Gale was bigger, but this she-bear was fierce. He recognized her immediately as Cedar. She had no intention of letting her catch go. She roared loudly in his face and bared her white icicle teeth at him.

"That's time!" Weston called from the trees. "Sun's down."

Cedar huffed and shoved Gale away from her, stealing the fish in the same motion. Gale stood on his hind legs, watching the exaggerated waggle of Cedar's fluffy ass as the water conformed around her. She held her head high and chomped down on the flailing fish to quiet it. Sassy as fuck. He didn't know if that irritated him or endeared him. It should have been neither. She was a *Trinity* Shifter.

Gale grunted and went back to the riverbank, the section where the fishing house stood. Everyone met there to change back into their human forms and reclaim their clothes before freezing to death. Gale made sure to thoroughly shake the icy water off his oily fur first. The other polar bears did the same. Then he shifted back, his human skin remaining mostly dry. He rolled his broad shoulders back and cracked his neck to stave off the chill creeping into his bones. He was about to reach down for his clothes when Cedar walked up to him, hands on her defined hips. Her skin was covered in goosebumps, but she apparently didn't give a damn. She wasn't wearing a lick of clothing.

"You tried to steal my fish," she said.

Nudity wasn't weird in Eurio. It couldn't be with an all-shifter community—sans Austin. The fact Gale grew up with it didn't change how his body reacted to this she-bear, though. What was it about her exactly? Physical beauty, she had it. So did many others. Her personality was refreshing. Ah, and her damn arousal. He could smell it again. He could taste it in the air like sweet honey on his tongue. It was all because of that. Her bear wouldn't stop calling to his.

"I went for it before you had it," Gale replied. He grabbed his clothes and made sure to get his bottom half covered before anything else. He was getting hard. "Besides, I let you have it in the end."

She scoffed, "Let me have it? I *took* it."

"Get dressed, Cedar."

She folded her arms, covering her perfect breasts, though it was not her intention. She was giving him the stink eye. "Fine." She turned around, flipping her long black hair behind her as she grabbed her clothes and got dressed. She was the last one to don her coat. Gale caught Mateo smirking at him. His parents were looking at him too. He couldn't decipher their looks, but he knew they smelled the arousal in the air. There was nothing he could do about that. At least Ike's nose couldn't quite register what that scent meant. He was still a kid after all. Besides, this was all Cedar's fault.

"Show me what you got," Weston said. He inspected everyone's catches with a straight face, but his eyes grew wide when he saw Cedar's. "Well, I'll be damned. That's quite a haul, Mongoyak."

She puffed out her chest and held her chin just a little higher. "They don't call me the Fishing Queen for nothing."

"Clearly. You win. The only other shifter who came close to you was Gale."

"Dad!" Ike exclaimed, tugging on Gale's coat sleeve. "Will Cedar teach me how to fish?"

"Go ask her," Gale replied, more than a little unhappy at the prospect.

Ike took a deep breath, stilling his wild energy. He walked up to Cedar like a little gentleman, making sure not to crowd her, to be respectful like he was taught, and asked, "You're amazing. Will you teach me how to fish?"

"Okay, Isaac. I'm sure I can teach you a thing or two your dad hasn't."

"Just Ike. And my dad didn't teach me how to fish. Papa Blanc did."

Gale grimaced but quickly covered it up. "You won, Cedar. That means you're in charge of preparing dinner. Put us to work."

"I know exactly what I want," she said. "But I'll need a few key helpers."

"Me," Ike said. He didn't make any big movements, but his hands trembled at his sides. It was like he kept all of his excitement inside of his palms, and it was fighting to go free.

"Thank you, Ike. I want *Gale* to help too. You'll be my leads."

No thanks, Gale thought. He was about to protest, but Ike spoke up. "Please, Dad," he said.

Gale had the urge to look away, to hide the vulnerability that could be exposed with eye contact. "You really want me to?" he asked.

"Please."

After rubbing the back of his head, Gale gave a quick nod. It wasn't like he had a choice anyway. Cedar was in charge of dinner.

"We'll all help of course," Weston said. "Let's head to the Lodge. Bring your kills."

Mateo and Ike bumped fists as Mateo walked past with his mate and the other shifters, leaving Cedar, Gale, and Ike to take up the rear.

"How *did* you catch so many fish?" Gale asked.

Cedar grinned. "These bad boys of course." She flexed her arm and used her opposite hand to pat her bicep.

Gale rolled his eyes.

"I can teach you and Ike," she offered. "It's mostly practice—and my excellent instincts. It helps that I have a love for food." She patted her belly and purposefully stuck it out more so it appeared larger. He hated that she did things that tugged at the corners of his lips, begging him to smile. He coughed to hide it. Then Cedar bumped her hip against him. "It's not a crime to smile, Gale."

"I'll try to remember that," he said, and Ike took his hand. His grip was loose at first, but Gale rewarded him by squeezing. That must have been the right thing to do because his cub beamed. He was as radiant as his mother, so bright it was hard to look at him, but at least Gale could revel in his warmth. Maybe one day he could look at the *Sun* without it blinding him.

CHAPTER 6

THE KITCHEN SMELLED LIKE heaven. Most of the dishes showcased fish, but the wolves had managed to catch some elk too. the Lodge was a communal place and where the majority of Eurio's food was kept. It had electricity too, making cooking convenient. Cedar was glad the Lodge was also stocked with herbs and frozen veggies and fruits. She could put all of her skills to use here, and she did. These shifters had no idea what they were doing. The way Ike's face lit up when he took a taste of Cedar's veggie and berry soup reminded her how much she loved cooking. Heck, and why was this kid so cute? Maybe it was because he was a novelty. She hadn't had much to do with kids in a while. With her life choices and all. Man, but she liked the way this kid looked up to her. She was pretty damn awesome, though. She totally deserved it.

She took a taste of her soup too. Flavor burst on her tongue like fireworks. Oh, yeah. It was just as good as she remembered. It was hard to think she stopped putting in the effort to make good food in exchange for time. She never wanted to eat another TV dinner again. It didn't compare. But it wasn't just the taste of home-made food she had missed. It was people to share it with. Yeah, she was part of Trinity, but she lived alone, moving from apartment to apartment depending on where Trinity wanted her. Her life was rather solitary. She hadn't thought much about home in a while, not since before coming back to Alaska, but maybe she was a bit homesick.

"It's so good, Cedar," Ike said and snuck another spoonful.

She couldn't blame him. Hell, she joined him. "Right?" she said. "So delicious."

"Save some for the others," Gale said, stealing the pot.

"He's right, Ike." Cedar sighed. "Let's help take the rest of this food out."

The dining room was huge with several long tables set up to accommodate everyone. All the food occupied one table, and shifters were already lined up, taking empty plates and piling them high.

"Shifters eat a lot in general," Weston commented, "but you're going to get us eating more."

"My pleasure." Cedar curtsied, though she wasn't wearing a dress or skirt of any sort; it was sweaters and jeans all the way if she didn't have to dress up. She gave Ike a friendly tap. "You were an excellent helper."

"I don't know what to eat." The cub's eyes darted back and forth. Just when he'd settle his gaze on one thing, he'd slowly move on to the next and over again in an endless loop.

"Why not take a little bit of everything?"

The cub must have liked that idea, because that was exactly what he did.

When Cedar's plate was piled as high as she could get it, she vowed to come back for seconds. She looked around the room and picked a table with an empty space. She thought she'd end up sitting alone, but Ike slid in beside her. "May I eat with you, Cedar?"

"I think you're supposed to ask that before you sit down."

"Sorry."

"I'm kidding. You can totally eat with me." She didn't add that it was a relief. She seemed to be fitting into Eurio well enough, but she wasn't sure how much the shifters here liked her—especially Gale. She took a bite of sheefish. It was perfectly prepared; the meat was tender, flaky goodness.

She was so involved in her food, she nearly missed another shifter who sat down across from her. When she looked up, she almost choked. It was none other than Gale. He had hardly anything on his plate. He had sheefish like her for his main course and one measly salad side.

"Looking pretty sad there." She pointed her fork at his disgraceful dinner. "I promise it all tastes fabulous."

"I never said it didn't. I'm not very hungry."

Since when was a bear of any sort *not* hungry?

Cedar intended to go back to her food. She really did. But Gale kept watching her. And it was like his gaze alone was enough to get her excited. She refused to squeeze her thighs together in response. Ike was oblivious, thank spirits, but Gale knew exactly what was going on. It wasn't like she could hide her arousal from an adult male polar bear. Did he want to use her attraction to pressure her into something? His eyes were smoldering.

She cleared her throat. "Do you have something you want to say?"

Though she had caught a whiff of Gale's own arousal and his half-hard cock back at the riverbank, he didn't seem interested in exploring this attraction— which was probably smart of him. It was also good for her. *He's trouble, Cedar,* she reminded herself.

If Gale did have something to say, he didn't get the chance to say it. Mateo slid in to sit next to him. At least Weston was gracious enough to give her a rundown of all the names of the shifters present for the Hunt. She had seen some pictures and files at her briefing, but she preferred not to assume anything. Except, knowing what she knew about Gale made that hard to do. The fact was she did know things she shouldn't about these shifters. She had preformed ideas and opinions about them even though she didn't personally know them, like Gale being a polar bear just waiting to go Berserker at the loss of his mate. But it had been years since Iris died. If he was going to go Berserker, wouldn't he have done it by now?

Gale stood up, but Mateo grabbed his arm. "Sit down, old bear. You haven't even touched your food." The wolf shifter scowled. "I sound like you. When did that happen?"

Gale gave a dry laugh.

"You better not be leaving because I sat down by you. You mad I moved out?"

Austin appeared next. Mateo scooted over to make room, bumping against Gale who reluctantly scooted over as well and sat back down. Mateo's arm went around his mate's waist, and he pressed a kiss to Austin's freckled neck. It was a lingering kiss, and Cedar saw tongue. Oh, hell. She could feel the heat from here. She wasn't the one getting neck kisses, but she sure wouldn't have minded it—from Gale. The soft smile on Austin's face had to mean it felt good. Really good.

When Mateo stopped, Austin's face was red. He fixed his glasses and cleared his throat. "Uh, hey again, Cedar."

Cedar waved.

"This is the best food I've ever tasted. Are you going to stay here for a while?"

"Hey, whatever I can do to spread the appreciation of good food, I will. Even if I don't stick around for a while, I'll offer some lessons before I leave."

"That's very generous of you."

"Nothing makes food better than sharing."

"I know what you mean. It's too bad Mateo is a picky eater."

The wolf shifter growled. "Just because I don't like those gross oatmeal raisin cookies doesn't mean I'm picky."

Austin replied by planting a kiss on his cheek. "I still love you."

"You better. You've got my scent. And my mark."

Okay. These two were disgustingly sweet. They were warm too. Cedar liked Eurio and its residents well enough. They were easy to talk to and felt genuine. Sharing dinner with them made her food taste a million times better than it would have on its own, but she missed her family badly. It had been too long. She hadn't thought about them for too long. She needed to drop them a line for Christmas. Her parents, brothers, sisters… It was kind of crazy how she let her new life with Trinity consume her so much she had ultimately left them behind. *But for fucking real,* she thought. *If they wanted to keep in touch, they could have done me the basic courtesy of going to the nearest city to send me a letter.*

There was no use dwelling on it. She left on bad terms. She knew her clan wouldn't bend. That was why things had ended up this way. She was stubborn too, but maybe being stubborn was only worth so much. If it kept her estranged from her family, maybe it wasn't worth much at all. Would going back to visit mean more fighting, or would they be able to set aside their differences?

"Mateo," Gale said.

"Yeah?"

"Have you seen Yuri or Lance?"

"Over there."

Cedar followed Mateo's pointing finger straight to the Lenkovs. Lance was properly dressed now. The dark circles under Yuri's eyes weren't as prominent. He had also trimmed his beard. "That's a good sign," she said.

Gale grunted.

Damn, if he wasn't grumpy. After closing her eyes to stop herself from rolling them, Cedar glanced up at the ceiling and the visible beams of wood crisscrossing to hold up the steeply angled roof. The wood was nice, the architecture sound, but this place was missing something big time. It was plain as hell. Surely a cheerier atmosphere would lighten any dreary moods. If she was forced to stay cooped up in all this drab every-building-looks-the-sameness, she would feel sick too.

She turned to Gale and asked, "Do you guys have something against decorating?"

"Not much point to it," he said.

"Some Christmas lights? A Christmas tree? Just one little thing would make this place feel livelier. Cozier too."

Gale stood up, his nearly full plate in hand. "Decorate the entire town if you want to, Cedar. I won't stop you." He escaped the table. Weston intercepted him before he left the building, taking his food. And then Gale was gone. It was like he couldn't get out of the Lodge fast enough.

"He always does that," Ike said.

"He doesn't eat anything and leaves without a word?" Cedar asked.

"Yeah. That. Mama Blanc says he's sad. Sometimes when we're sad, we need to be alone."

"When I'm sad, I don't want to be alone."

Ike stared at the door his father disappeared through. His face was unreadable, his lips set in their natural curve. His eyes held no answers because the windows were obstructed by a sea of clouds.

In the briefing before Cedar left, she learned Gale was still pestering Trinity about the case concerning Iris and her team. They promised to let him know if they found anything out, but he kept asking anyway. His mind wasn't in Eurio. It was on his dead mate.

Years later, it was still on his dead mate.

"Don't worry, Ike," Cedar said. "I'll stay here with you, and we can go back to your house when you're ready to. You call the shots, all right?"

The cub nodded. "Thanks, Cedar." He took another bite of his food. His plate was empty aside from the juices left behind, which he insisted on licking away until the ceramic plate had had a thorough tongue bath; it was left spotless.

To be a kid, Cedar thought.

"I'm done," Ike announced. He high-fived Mateo as he left the table, and Cedar followed him. "We gotta wash off our dishes."

"So responsible," Cedar praised. She did as the little guy instructed. It was amusing being told how to wash a dish and dry it by a seven-year-old, but she didn't laugh. She took the responsibility very seriously.

"Good job," Ike said once they had put away their clean plates.

"Thank you, Ike. You're a good teacher."

He nodded like this was an obvious fact.

"Ready to go home?"

He shook his head. "Teach me to fish, Cedar." Then he added, remembering his manners, "Please."

She laughed. "Sure. I think we have some time for

fishing. What's the dark got on a couple of polar-bear shifters?"

"Nothing!"

"Right answer. Now, let's bring your dad home the biggest fish we can find. And you'll catch it all on your own."

Ike rocked on his feet, though he seemed to be doing his best to stay still. "Let's go." He grinned and pumped his fist. "Let's go!"

CHAPTER 7

GALE'S BIG WHITE PAWS left sizable indents in the snow. He huffed and puffed hot streams of air from his black nose, nostrils opening and closing. It was dark, but his night vision worked well enough for him to maneuver through the uneven terrain. He stuck close to the river, following the current. It would lead him home eventually.

His head was pounding, pulsing. When he looked up to the sky, the stars were too numerous. They coalesced and sprang out in neon colors, multiplied, scattered. Fell. And he followed.

Slowly, Gale blinked his eyes. He wasn't on his feet. His big belly was flat against the cold earth, snow compacted into a hard sheet of ice. He hardly felt it between his thick coat and the warm buzz of the booze he had drunk way too much of in the small human town nearest to Eurio. It was several miles away, which usually gave him enough time to clear his head before returning home, but not tonight. He had overdone it.

After getting wasted, he had stumbled out of the bar. He was thinking too clearly in his human form even though he shouldn't have been able to. He called out to his bear when the spruces engulfed him. It was easier not to think in this form, but even his intoxicated bear was thinking too much. No, it wasn't thinking. He was aching. He couldn't get the pain to stop.

He grunted and stayed put, too tired to get off his belly. His chest ached too much, and his breathing was labored. He was almost convinced he had an open wound, his heart blown to bits. This was what it had felt like when he had first learned Iris was dead. The pain hadn't been this intense in a while.

Gale tried to get back to his feet, but his paws wouldn't work. So, he resorted to crawling. He dug down deep into the snow and found purchase on the rocks underneath. With a ridiculous amount of effort, he pulled himself closer to the river. Maybe the water would wake him up.

Maybe it would drown him.

Agonizing paw forward after agonizing paw forward, Gale made it to the water's edge. He shimmied out onto the ice, chin leading the way as he skimmed across the slippery surface. Then there was a crack. The ice underneath him shifted, and he fell again.

Water rattled his skull and muffled his ears, and light shimmered on the moving surface above him. It faded into nothing as he sank deeper. The stars blinked out. His eyes closed. He inhaled a gallon of water, cement in his lungs. It would be so easy to let this be it. It could all be over. Just. Like. This.

His lungs screamed at him. They begged him to use his powerful limbs to claw and scratch to the surface, to breach the poison killing him.

But what was the point?

You have a cub.

He was an absent father, but Ike smiled when Gale spent time with him. Ike kept begging for his attention because he still wanted him. Needed him.

White tendrils crept into the edges of Gale's vision as his eyes snapped open. Fire ignited inside of his stomach, and it grew. It planted itself in his veins, ripped through them. He was engulfed in freezing water, but he was burning.

Then he exploded.

Droplets burst from the river like shooting stars. The water sizzled and bubbled as white-hot energy burned into it, disrupting its natural flow. Suddenly, there was air. Gale gasped. His lungs greedily drinking in the oxygen. He stood on his back legs, a dry riverbed underneath him. He held his paws up to his face and saw that they were glowing; they almost hurt to look at because they were so bright. Water rushed downstream but hastily darted out to either side of him. What hit him evaporated in seconds. He was leaking fire. Steam followed the river's flow and captured the light he was emitting like roiling clouds filled with angry pulses of lightning. It got brighter and brighter until Gale knew he was going to explode again.

BOOM!

The water buzzed in his ears like a swarm of bees. Then something slammed into him like a ton of bricks. He fell over, facefirst into the river current resuming its natural course. After the water calmed some and became more predictable, Gale swam to shore. He shook the water off his coat and looked down at his paws. They weren't glowing anymore, but his veins were still hot. The energy stemmed from his belly and again reached out to his limbs. The dark pads on his paws lightened first. Brighter and brighter still, he lit up like a miniature sun.

He expelled a low growl and tamped down the Sunlight growing inside of him. It all clicked into place now. He finally understood what was happening to him. This was Solsis. Iris had explained it to him before. She had even shown him. All shifters belonged to one of the Celestial Trinity and a specific branch of, well, magic. Polar-bear shifters like Gale were categorized as Sun Shifters. Most of the time, this information had little to do with a shifter's life, and most shifters outside of Trinity either knew nothing about this or only knew bits and pieces. But there were some shifters who could tap into hidden power beyond shifting. Solsis was the Sun's hidden power. It was explosive, dangerous, and hard to control. Gale had never accessed it before tonight. So why now? What had changed?

His brain was fuzzy like radio static. The Solsis ignited again, starting in his belly. He was burning so hot, this time he thought he might breathe fire. He closed his eyes, determined to make it stop before he exploded again. Then this flopping noise caught his attention. Fish lay strewn about in the snow, a result of his previous explosion. Some of them had their flesh burned off and were very dead. Others were doing their best to return to the water. But they eventually slowed, unable to breathe.

The Solsis wouldn't stop. It grew stronger, and Gale's paws lit up. His fur was fire.

He dove back into the water. If he couldn't control this power, the least he could do was make sure he didn't somehow set the snowy forest on fire. As the dark water cradled him in its icy embrace, he closed his eyes, curled up into a ball, and exploded again.

He prayed to the Sun, to anything that might listen, and he asked it to stop.

He begged it to stop.

BOOM!

There it was again. Cedar was running for her life through the black and white spruces. Her heart was pounding in time with the explosions that kept following her, and she couldn't take much more. She didn't know what kind of monster was chasing her, but it was something big, mean, and deadly. The whole forest was up in flames.

BOOM!

The ground underneath Cedar groaned as it opened its yawning mouth to consume her.

Then she gasped awake.

Sweat dripped down her brow. It was dark, nothing but Moonlight soft against the curtains of her window.

"Just a nightmare," she muttered. She sighed and lay back down. She rolled over, closed her eyes, and tried to ignore the ringing in her eardrums.

BOOM!

A blast of blinding light burned through her eyelids, and she jumped out of bed. That sound wasn't from a dream at all. It was Solsis, and she had a sinking feeling she knew exactly who was using it.

Quickly, before exiting the house in a rush, she looked in on Ike. He was fast asleep. Apparently, the kid could sleep through a freight train right outside his window, but it was just as well. He'd be safer here. Next, she knocked on Gale's door. She didn't wait for a response and let herself inside. Just like when she and Ike had come home after a very successful fishing trip, Gale was absent. They had to take that huge burbot Ike caught and store it in the icebox.

Ike told her it was normal for Gale to be gone. She hadn't liked that. It didn't seem good for a seven-year-old boy to be home alone all the time.

BOOM!

Cedar steeled herself for what she was about to face. She forced her boots on her feet, donned her coat, scarf, hat, gloves, and she left the house. Instead of admitting her fear, she wrote off the shivers going up and down her spine as a result of the ice and snow biting her skin. The Sun had been down for hours, and the world was much colder for it. It was just the cold.

BOOM!

This time Cedar saw it with open eyes, and it burned. It was like a huge-ass flash bomb had just been set off near the Tanana River. At least she knew what direction she needed to head in. She picked up the pace as she sensed other shifters heading in the same direction. Some were hidden in the trees while others were just coming out of the few scattered cabins she passed as she ran. The sour scent of fear and panic was so potent she could taste it. They didn't know what was going on. It was more important than ever that she got to the source of these Solsis Bursts first.

She wasn't a peacekeeper, but she could use Solsis, and maybe that little extra detail on her résumé was the reason Trinity decided she was up to handling Eurio all on her own; they had to have factored in the possibility of this happening. Right now, however, she wished she had had some peacekeeper training. She had been through self-protection classes, but she didn't have field experience, and she was starting to worry that she might be out of her depth.

Cedar's human form was not the most athletic, but the bear inside of her made up for that. She got to the riverbank before anyone else. She passed the fishing shanty and continued against the river's current. She was close now. There was a faint glow coming from inside the water and ice. It was Gale. Water roared around him as if he were a boulder blocking its way, repelled by his oily fur and the out-of-control Solsis enveloping his entire body.

"Gale!" she shouted. "What are you doing?"

His big blocky head jerked over in her direction. His eyes were bloodshot, and he grunted, trying to tell her something, but communicating with their animals was not as easy or as fine of an art as using actual words. It came down to feeling, and Cedar could sense Gale's confusion. If she had to guess, he had stumbled upon this power by accident. That was better than the alternative. If his mind was still intact, she could get through to him.

"Come out of the water," she said, doing her best

to keep her voice level. "You just have to calm down, and it'll stop."

Cedar's ears twitched, picking up movement beyond Gale. She held out her hands to stop whoever was behind her and turned around to see Weston, Cary, and Mateo. She slowly shook her head and put her pointer finger to her lips. She needed them to leave this to her. Mateo was jittery, barely containing a snarl, and looked like he was ready to burst. It was a good thing he wasn't a Sun Shifter. He wouldn't actually explode like a miniature sun if he lost it. Thankfully, Weston and Cary held him back, though.

"Gale," Cedar tried again.

Gale roared and shook his head. He dove under the water as the light intensified to the point it made Cedar's eyes blurry and exploded again. Water burst into steam while sizable amounts of it fled, still liquid or ice, and splashed onto the riverbank, soaking Cedar and lightly spraying the wolves behind her.

Sopping wet, Cedar's clothes were quite useless. She struggled with removing them from her person, teeth chattering the entire time before she was naked and able to call on her bear without ripping everything to shreds. Her shift was smooth. Though her bones cracked and broke as her body reformed and became much larger, she was in tune with her feral half. She was comfortable, and her newly sprouted fur fought away the cold in a way her bare skin never could.

She plopped down onto all four paws and quietly walked closer to the river's edge. So far, so good. She waded in the river as it resumed its normal course, pelting Gale with pent-up force now that he was no longer turning water to steam. He was almost taken under by the ferocity of it, but he stayed above water, gasping for air. He growled a warning at her, big black lips curled back to reveal a sharp set of teeth. Cedar ignored him. She kept a steady pace forward against the current.

As she came closer, she let out soft grunts, doing her best to appear passive. The last thing she wanted to do was rile him up more. But his body was charging up again. Like those dimmable lightbulbs, the light coming off of him just kept amping up as if someone was twisting its knob to the highest setting.

If she was being perfectly honest, Cedar had no idea what she was doing or what she should do. She was just doing something. According to the information she got in that briefing before she had left, none of the shifters in Eurio knew how to use Celestial Magic. Whatever happened here was dependent on her. It was her responsibility to keep everyone in Eurio safe.

She wasn't stupid, though. To protect herself, she called on Solsis as well. The flames started in her core, a little simmer, and they grew larger, expanding through her body as she directed it to engulf her. Gale moved back against the current, trying to keep away from her, but he didn't try hard enough. He was exhausted, using Solsis Burst after Solsis Burst, and he was barely holding the water back. Cedar stopped in front of him and dug her back legs into the riverbed to stay planted there even after Gale would inevitably lose to the river. She held out her paw and grunted again, hoping Gale would understand. He hesitantly touched her paw with his own. His paw was burning. He was leaking Solsis while she kept it safely contained, but the light they both emitted was beyond blinding.

Cedar closed her eyes to save her retinas and reeled the power in. The flames grew smaller and smaller until that little simmering match at her core was snuffed out completely. Gale's paw wasn't burning her anymore. A fierce wave of water tried to take her down, but she held fast. When she opened her eyes, she was relieved to see that Gale was following her lead. He could sense what she was doing through that simple touch connecting them. The light vanished, and all of the volatile energy was contained. For now, it was gone entirely.

Gale huffed his exhaustion. He looked bad, sick even. Cedar lowered her paw and pressed her nose to Gale's. He drew back, nostrils flaring. He stood tall on his hind legs, much taller than her. She gently pressed her forehead into his bobbing chest. She stayed like that until his breathing resumed its natural ebb and flow. They were steadfast, two boulders in the river, but it was time to resume their life as polar-bear shifters.

Cedar took a deep breath, moved back, and pointed to the riverbank. Gale huffed but otherwise followed her lead without complaint. Weston and Cary were waiting with warm blankets in hand; they must have grabbed them while Cedar was calming Gale down. Mateo was alone in his own space, slumped against a tree trunk, eyes flickering yellow to brown and back to yellow again. His teeth were bared as he fought a shift. Gale locked eyes with him, grunted softly, and the inner-fight ceased. Mateo let out a shuddering sigh as he pushed off the tree trunk and his eyes finally settled on brown.

After thoroughly shaking off excess water, Gale and Cedar both shifted. Weston and Cary wasted no time covering them with the warm blankets.

"You should get home before you catch a cold," Weston said. "That is, if you think you should go home." He looked at Cedar.

"Gale's okay," she said. "Besides, I'll be there to keep him from exploding again." However, warm drinks might be in order by the time they returned, and they weren't walking back all that way in their naked human skins.

"And I thought I was dangerous," Mateo said. He came forward and rested his forehead on Gale's shoulder. Gale grabbed the back of Mateo's head and ran his hand over Mateo's buzzed hair. "Sorry for making you worry. It's fine now. Thanks for coming to get me, though."

"You got it. Do you need me to come back with you?"

"No. You probably left Austin in a hurry. He'll be worried about you."

Mateo winced.

"Go back home. I'll be fine."

"You smell like cheap booze," Mateo informed.

"Feel like cheap booze." Gale chuckled. He wobbled on his feet, and Cedar caught him, accidentally dropping her blanket in the process. She did her best not to think about his hard muscles, how he felt even through the blanket he managed to keep hold of. Her body didn't do the same. Her pussy clenched like a little beast that had been starved for far too long. This was not what she had expected from her first night in Eurio.

CHAPTER 8

GETTING GALE HOME TURNED out to be more of a hassle than Cedar was anticipating. At least in the form of her bear, she didn't mind his weight as much—but she still minded. He was heavy. And he was drunk.

She had to keep him going in a straight line, but he fought her with each step they took. Every time she looked over her furry shoulder at him, she was met with unseeing, bloodshot eyes. He huffed like they were hiking up a steep trail. She growled at him at one point, demanding he get his shit together. It was the longest walk ever, but they made it to Gale's cabin in one piece.

Exhausted, Cedar shoved Gale off of her and shifted. She shivered as the cold ate through her skin. When she looked back, she expected Gale to be shifted as well, but he was still a big, swaying polar bear. He fell in the snow, ass-first, and then he dropped forward onto his belly, chin-first. His breaths grew deeper, and his eyes closed. Did he just pass out? He couldn't possibly be planning on sleeping right there.

"Oh no, you don't," Cedar said. "You get up right now and shift," she put her hands on her hips, shuddered, and then hugged her arms around her middle, "or I'm going in without you."

Gale's eyes opened and closed slowly. When they opened again, they rested on Cedar. He huffed and pushed himself up onto his hind legs and shifted like Cedar told him to. It was an agonizing change. It started with his fur receding, and then his bones re-shaping. The grimace wrinkling his snout stayed as a wrinkled human nose when his shift was complete. He pressed his hand to his forehead and winced like he had an awful headache—which he probably did.

Cedar tried not to think about his ripped body. She did a good job of not thinking about it as a polar bear, maybe because he was making her work too hard.

But now they were standing here, together again, naked again. The cold sank through the soles of her feet, and all she could see were Gale's rippling muscles. She was mesmerized by the way every inch of his massive arm moved as one fluid unit when he dropped his hand back down to his side. Then her eyes were on his narrow hips. Then that thin line of hair from his bellybutton down to that thick patch of dark pubic hair and his half-erect dick. Did she get to take credit for that?

Focus, Cedar, she told herself and gestured to the door. "You first."

Gale didn't argue. He led the way inside and didn't stop. It was up to Cedar to be responsible, to close the door, to quickly listen and check that Ike was still sleeping soundly. The cabin was warm enough, so she didn't feel like she was freezing to death anymore, but she should probably find some clothes. She looked at Gale leaning against the door frame of his room, like he was considering if he wanted to go in or not, and cursed this job. She had become a glorified babysitter. His eyes were drooping. He was going to fall and hit his head. Clothes would have to wait a minute longer.

"Gale, you can't sleep here."

He groaned and kept his eyes closed. Cedar rolled

up her imaginary sleeves and tested her human biceps by giving them a tight squeeze. Then she braced herself. She moved forward, looped an arm around Gale's waist, and grabbed the arm closest to her, forcing Gale to wrap it around her shoulder and lean on her instead. He ended up sort of falling onto her. She groaned under his weight, and her legs protested, but she managed to take a step forward, and Gale managed to follow her lead. She was not thinking about his hot skin on hers. Not at all.

The journey across Gale's room should have been short. It didn't take that many steps to get from the doorway to his bed, but drunk Gale was very done cooperating; he was determined to sleep standing.

"Come on, Gale. Just a little farther," Cedar said, more for herself than him. She tightened her grasp around his waist, ignoring how nice his skin felt against hers. His arm began to slip off her shoulder, he sank into her, and his hand brushed against one of her large breasts. Her face heated up. She couldn't believe the ridiculousness of this whole situation. And now her traitorous body was on fire. That one little touch—accidental touch—got her way more excited than it should have.

"Down you go." Cedar did her best to maneuver

Gale, but she couldn't get his heavy arm off from around her shoulders. So when he bellyflopped down onto the bed, he ended up taking her with him. Now she was trapped underneath his arm and part of his chest. It was at an uncomfortable angle too; she was hanging half-off the bed.

"Gale!" she protested. "This is absolutely ridiculous." But he was already snoring.

Cedar wiggled and shimmied her way out from underneath him. She probably touched almost every inch of him by the time she was through. She was quite sure her hand touched his dick. She was red-faced and worked up when she was standing again. She sighed. And she stared. She should've left then. Instead, she listened to his soft snoring, watched the slow rise and fall of his chest. She found a blanket tossed aside and covered him with it. She didn't know if she did it as a kindness or if she did it for herself.

"Spirits," she murmured. She was turned on high and melting.

She squeezed her thighs together, resisting the urge to touch herself, to answer the call of her need. The room's door was wide open. Although Ike seemed to be a heavy sleeper, she was not going to deal with any of that. She was not going to touch herself while watching Gale sleep! She bit her lower lip.

"Okay, Cedar. You've more than overstayed your welcome. Enough."

She left and closed Gale's door, allowing him his privacy before heading for her own room. Clothes were the first thing on her agenda. When she was in the safety of her own room, with the door closed, she searched through her meager belongings. But her hand found its way in between her legs anyway. That buzzing energy in her core wouldn't leave, and it wasn't Solsis.

CHAPTER 9

IT WAS EARLY MORNING. Cedar only knew that because she looked at the time on her laptop. She couldn't tell by the Sun because there wasn't any Sun here half the time. That was Alaska for you. When she lived in other states, like Texas, it was almost like living in another, much warmer, world. Before Trinity, she hadn't known about Solsis. She hadn't missed the Sun like she did since returning to Alaska. But, right now, the Sun could stay down. She wanted to sleep.

She was up most of the night fixing all the inconsistencies she could find between Eurio's current records and the information given to Trinity. Mostly, things were up to date. It wasn't like Gale and Weston had been giving false information. They just hadn't been giving enough.

Cedar sighed, sinking back in her chair. It was seven o'clock. Could she get away with going to bed?

She groaned when she heard a door closing. She didn't want it to be her responsibility, but Gale had been a mess last night, so it was probably best if she investigated.

She went to the kitchen, where she smelled fish. She was expecting Gale, but it was Ike. The seven-year-old was using the stove and frying up some of the burbot they had caught last night. The rest was on the counter. He had flayed it all by himself too, like he'd done this a million times before. For all Cedar knew, maybe he had. She hadn't had him flay anything when they made dinner at the Lodge. Clearly, she had made a mistake.

"Morning, Ike."

"Morning, Cedar. Want some?"

"Only if you're going to season it properly."

Ike shrugged.

"Do you have seasonings here? Herbs? Veggies?"

Ike shook his head. "Not really. Just at the Lodge."

Since getting assigned to stay in Gale's cabin yesterday, Cedar hadn't taken the opportunity to snoop around. She had gotten straight to work instead, but looking at the kitchen now, she was appalled by how bare it was. She opened and inspected all the cupboards. Most of them had nothing but dust in them. She found only four plates, a handful of silverware, and a couple of cups. It was insanely minimalist. the Lodge had given Cedar some hope for this town, but Gale's cabin dashed it all away again.

"All right, Ike. Fry me up the best fish you can. I'm sure it'll taste wonderful."

"Okay," he said as he eagerly got to work, laying out more thin slices of firm white flesh on the pan.

Cedar took a moment to appreciate it by sniffing the air. "Are you going to make some for your dad, too?"

"No. He's probably not home."

Cedar frowned. He just assumed his father wasn't home, and he dug into this prize fish they caught without showing it off first? He didn't even check his father's room? She didn't like that. "Doesn't he take you to school?" she asked.

"When he remembers. Mostly, I go by myself. I don't like to be late. But he gets mad sometimes. Not like angry mad, the quiet mad, you know?"

"I think I do." Cedar thought about how dysfunctional Gale was last night. "Do you know if your dad drinks alcohol a lot? You know, the stuff that makes him lose his balance and maybe act a little funny? Mad even?"

"Sometimes every day? Sometimes not very often? I don't know."

There wasn't any booze in the icebox, but Cedar wondered. Maybe she needed to ask someone else about Gale's behavior. Perhaps Weston would know, seeing as he was the other Alpha in charge of Eurio. She didn't know why that title was shared between them when Gale was clearly struggling. Why didn't his mother or father take his place? Was he holding on to it with no intention of stepping down? Was he thrust into this position because Iris was his mate? That seemed entirely too possible. Cedar didn't know Gale well at all, personally anyway, and he had a funny way of showing he cared, but she was pretty sure that he did care. No, she *knew* he did. He wouldn't have checked on the Lenkovs' if he hadn't. He was genuinely worried about them.

"You good to watch the food? You do this all the time, right?" Cedar asked.

"Yep," Ike said as he flipped the meat over with a

spatula.

"I'm going to check on your dad real quick. I'll be back."

Ike nodded, concentrating on the sizzling pan and nothing else.

Cedar considered knocking on Gale's door but settled for opening it quietly instead. As she figured, Gale was snoring deeply, fast asleep. She left without a word.

She returned to the kitchen, where Ike gave her a plate with a big cut of fish. Cedar was impressed with how well it was cooked, browned just so, tender and juicy. She took a bite and appreciated the texture, the pure taste of burbot without seasonings to enhance it. Teach this kid how to enhance flavor and he'd be a force to fear.

"This is great!" Cedar exclaimed. "You didn't tell me you were already a bona fide chef, Ike."

"It doesn't always turn out good," he admitted. His cheeks were a little red, eyes focused on his food as he took a bite. His eyes lit up. "I did do good today!"

Cedar laughed. She had made up her mind years ago that she never wanted to have kids, but if she had a kid like Ike, she didn't think she'd mind. This kid was basically perfect.

And it wasn't that she didn't like kids.

"How about I walk with you to school today?" she asked. "And you can show me Weston's cabin on the way. I don't really know where he lives."

"Okay. I can take you to Weston's."

"I'm taking you to school after I know where it is, though."

"Okay."

When the polar bears finished breakfast, they both gathered what they needed for the day, bundled up, and left the quiet cabin and Gale behind. It snowed again at some point during the night. Ike and Cedar took turns leading and making tracks in the new snow. They changed their strides to make it harder for the one following to match their tracks. The extra effort made the walk take much longer, but they were too busy smiling and laughing to care.

"That's Weston's cabin," Ike said. It looked like every other cabin. Why wasn't Cedar surprised?

"Thanks, Ike. The school's still a little ways away, isn't it?"

"I can go by myself."

"Not a chance."

"Good morning." Cedar turned around to see Austin. "On your way to school, I hope."

"Yep. This kid is responsible. He got up on his own and even made breakfast."

"Glad to hear it." Austin smiled. "Class wouldn't be the same without you, Ike. Don't tell anybody else I said this, but you're my best participator. You make the other kids feel better. I couldn't run class without you."

Ike beamed. "Can I tell Mateo?"

"Mateo already knows. He's very proud of you. I'll tell him to tell you next time he sees you since he'll forget to otherwise."

Ike nodded. "We don't talk a lot." Then he growled. "We wrestle."

Austin laughed. "Yes. Yes, you do."

"How about you walk the rest of the way with Austin so I can talk to Weston and hopefully not trouble him too much. I don't know what his pack duties are like," Cedar said. "I'll pick you up when school is out. Three, right?"

"That's right," Austin said, patting Ike on the shoulder.

Ike shrugged and kicked at some snow. "Okay. Bye-bye, Cedar."

Cedar waved and watched Ike and Austin even after they set off in the opposite direction. Ike moved closer to Austin and looked up at him with a big grin on his face. He must have been telling the human something exciting. Ike bumped into Austin in that carefree and unguarded way cubs tended to act around those they trusted. He grabbed Austin's sleeve too, urging him closer. It was the sort of affection a cub gave family only. But it made sense. Austin was Mateo's mate, and Mateo was like a brother to Ike.

For having so many people who loved him, Ike had a lonely homelife.

Cedar walked up to Weston's cabin and knocked on the door. Cary answered it, holding a robe tight around her.

"Well, this is unusual," she said. "We don't often get visitors this early in the morning."

"Am I interrupting something?" Cedar asked. Then she wondered if she should've asked. What if she had interrupted something intimate between mates? Like sex. Her mind went back to Gale. Man, she certainly had one thing on her mind, didn't she? Just one thing.

"Not at all," Cary said. "We don't usually have company this early in the morning because we always run with the pack. Late into the night, I mean. Last night, we were all up late for a different reason, though."

Cedar pursed her lips. "Yep."

Cary laughed good-naturedly. "Weston and I had trouble sleeping after that. From the looks of yourself, you didn't get much sleep either. Was Gale trouble all night?"

"No, I just couldn't sleep after that fiasco." Her cheeks heated up. No way in hell was she going to say what had happened when she finally got him to his bed. Gale wouldn't remember it when he finally woke up anyway. She hoped.

"I see. Did you want Weston for something?"

"How could you tell?"

"A simple guess based on that laptop case you're lugging around."

"Got me."

"Come inside."

Cedar shed her layers and sat down on a plain wood-framed couch in the small living room.

Weston showed up a minute later.

Cary excused herself with, "I'll get some tea."

"She's just saying that so she doesn't have to deal with all this Trinity business," Weston said conspiratorially. "She is not the homemaker type."

Cedar laughed, hoping that was what she was supposed to do. She stood, they shook hands, and then

Weston gestured for her to sit back down.

"How's Gale?" he asked.

"Still sleeping. Between getting wasted and using all that energy, he might be out for a while. He'll be fine though," Cedar said.

"I hope so. Never seen anything like that. That was Solsis, wasn't it?"

"It was indeed. It's powerful stuff."

"No joke. Will he be doing that randomly now? You know, exploding…"

"If I wasn't here, that would be a possibility. But, since I am here, I'll help him get this under control. You don't have to worry." She left out adding, "Unless Gale is too far gone in his sorrow for his lost mate and is finally going Berserker like Trinity fears."

She cleared her throat. "Tell me about the Lenkovs. I know about Yuri's PWD. It's an unfortunate situation, but there's more than that, isn't there? I saw him yesterday. He wasn't doing well. Have the seizures gotten worse? Trinity is under the impression that he's stable."

"We have shifter healers, and we called a professional in, a trained neurologist. I believe we asked Trinity for references concerning that. It should even be in Trinity's records."

"Yes, that's true. And the seizures are just something Yuri has to live with, the PWD being the result."

"Exactly. So, what are you trying to get at?"

She clenched her fists. If there was no helping it, there was no helping it, but Eurio hadn't asked for the one resource Trinity had that no one else did. She needed to make sure Weston knew it was an option at least, since he should know far better than she did concerning the Lenkovs' situation. "What about a White Witch? They can do things shifter healers and doctors can't."

Weston pushed at the scar on his nose with his thumb.

"Well?" Cedar pressed.

"We haven't really considered it. Witches aren't welcome in Eurio."

Witches aren't welcome anywhere, Cedar thought. It was amazing that even those aligned with Trinity had issues with anyone different. Cedar had interacted with White Witches before, and they were perfectly normal other than the fact that they could use White Magic. It was different from Celestial Magic. The term magic might not have been an accurate word to use between the two either because Trinity had no idea where

White or Black Magic came from. They were something unique to witches, and none of Trinity's witches knew where their magic came from either. They just had it, produced it. Cedar only knew what she needed to. The study of magic of any sort was well beyond her.

She decided to drop this part of her conversation with Weston. She did what she needed to do. She made Weston aware. If Yuri was sick and needed help they couldn't give him, surely Weston or Gale would make the right choice. That was, if Gale's not-so-secret dislike for witches wasn't stronger than his concern for Yuri's well-being. Maybe Cedar needed to evaluate the Lenkovs on her own.

Cedar said, "Eurio is a shifter haven, a stopgap. The Hunt seems to be the only thing you encourage the shifters here to do when you should be requiring a lot more to get them back out into the world. To start, I think you could take advantage of the Hunt and do much more with it. What if, instead of a free-for-all, you had shifters work together in groups? How about building new cabins? You can teach the current residents new skills. They'll learn how to work together and trust each other rather than having the option to live in complete isolation—which isn't helpful.

"There's also the problem of how you deal with

new shifters. When Trinity sends shifters your way, they do a debrief to make sure they aren't a threat, but when you bring in shifters yourself, you don't even do that. That's a danger to Eurio, and it's unhelpful to the newcomers. You want to make a brighter future for these shifters, but if you don't know about their past, how can you? How can you take steps *now* to fix past traumas? If shifters are allowed to move in and do nothing, they'll stay and do nothing."

"That's quite a lecture," Weston said and scratched in between the braids hugging his scalp. "I promise we're not letting anyone isolate themselves to the degree you're implying. Gale and I always check in."

Cedar looked down at her hands. "Does Gale often come home plastered like that? Do you know what goes on in his house with Ike?"

"I don't live there, so I don't see everything. But yes, Gale has it rough. He's never laid a hand on his cub though, if that's what you're asking."

"No, he's just negligent," Cedar said more severely perhaps than she intended.

"He's been through a lot, but I'm sure you already know that. Also, Cedar, I understand you might not like how we do things. We don't do a formal debriefing, but we don't just let shifters in without some information on them. We're not incompetent. However, I agree some changes need to be made."

"Like your decision to bring Austin here without telling Trinity a thing." Cedar shook her head. "We're not the bad guys, Weston."

"That was Gale's idea, but he also didn't think Trinity would have a problem with it. We thought Trinity was too busy to pay us much mind anyway."

"See, that's why Trinity is worried. We just want to help each other. Nothing is too big or small in the dialogue that should be continuously running between Eurio and Trinity. Gale was right in assuming Trinity would have no problem with Austin living here, but we would have preferred to run a background check first, from another angle. Information is how we help each other. It's like relationship counseling. You know, when a couple is on the verge of getting a divorce, communication is always the place to start."

"Are you a counselor, Cedar?"

"Hell no." Then she muttered, "Watch too much TV." She cleared her throat. "But I know what I'm talking about here."

"Gale is strong for even being alive. Do you know what it's like to lose a mate?"

"No."

"Neither do I, but I was good friends with a wolf shifter who lost his mate to a rival pack. They were naturalist packs, living more like wolves than humans. He got away with slaughtering many in that rival pack, but he lost his life too in the end. He even left some pups behind."

"Berserker," Cedar said.

"That's right. Gale's not Berserker. He cares too much. He hasn't forgotten his cub, but he does have a broken heart that sorely needs mending. None of us know how to help him." Weston folded his arms. "Gale hasn't been interested in anybody for a long time, but he's interested in you."

Cedar faked a cough. "And what makes you think he's interested in me?"

"I really don't need to answer that, do I?"

Yeah, Cedar knew her attraction was no secret. It was normal for Gale's body to react the way it had. But, apparently, Weston was saying even that was abnormal for Gale since his mate died?

"What?" Cedar tried to play it off. "You don't have other single polar-bear shifters around here? Grizzlies? Black bears? Anything? Pretty sure I met some."

"We do, but he hasn't been interested in the slightest."

"I'm not going to fuck him and magically make his problems go away," Cedar grumbled.

"I didn't say that. I just thought it was interesting."

"And it's not that I wouldn't—he's hot as hell. He also has the cutest cub I've ever seen, and I've never even wanted cubs." Cedar pressed her fist against her mouth as if it were a plug. Why had she just run her mouth off like that? "Forget I said any of that. Let's get back to work."

"He's good, Cedar. If you want to give him a chance, if any part of you cares for him and Ike, give him a chance. And no, I'm not telling you to fuck him. I mean, it's none of my business. But you have a strong personality. You're not afraid to make things happen, and you're not afraid to confront him. You've been here just over a day, and you've already interacted with him more than anyone has—*really* interacted with him— since he went to grab Mateo back from Utah."

Cedar worried at her lower lip with her teeth before saying, "Let's get back to work."

CHAPTER 10

THE SUN FINALLY DECIDED to show face when Cedar returned to Gale's. She and Weston had finished their discussion, and Ike would be in school for a few hours more, which left Cedar with nothing to do. She went through the information Weston had and tidy up considerably before leaving, though. He seemed to take her suggestions seriously as well, so that was a good sign. She supposed it was all good timing too. Gale needed someone to check on him.

Cedar didn't see him when she walked through the cabin to drop her things off in her bedroom. She didn't hear anything either. It was dead silent. So, she walked up to Gale's door and knocked. When there was no reply, she opened the door quietly to find Gale exactly where she expected him to be. She would've been surprised if he had woken up and left the house after last night. Between the smell of cheap booze on his breath and all that energy, explosive Solsis, coursing through his body, he had to be dead tired. Hell, she was jittery and tired just from charging up once. Her fingers were tingling, that pins and needles tingling you get when your limb falls asleep. She hadn't expended the energy because she had forced it back down without any explosions involved. A fully executed Solsis Burst had bigger effects on the body, but she was feeling last night just fine.

Regardless of all that, it was time for Gale to wake up.

Cedar worried at her lower lip as she walked up to the sexy polar-bear shifter asleep in his bed. The blanket she had used to cover him last night had fallen to his waist. He was lying on his back, arms extended wide. She had a great view like this, and no one could fault her for staring. Gale was snoring softly, completely unaware. She felt that throbbing in her pussy again. Her eyes skimmed over his muscles, observing his defined pectorals and the lines of his abs. Those abs did not look real. They were too detailed, like they had been painted. She had the inappropriate urge to touch them, to see just how hard they were. She restrained herself because she was a respectful shifter, but then her eyes caught sight of the black hairs leading below Gale's bellybutton. The blanket hid the definition of anything beyond his hips, but she couldn't help staring at his happy-trail.

Her eyes settled on where Gale's sword was sheathed just under a blanket. She wiggled, rubbing her thighs together. Sword and sheath. She almost giggled. Her mind was fraying at the edges. She thought that was funny, dangerous, and hot all at once. God, but Gale did have quite a *sword* on him. She wondered how big it would be in all of its hard glory. More than once now, she had caught him half-hard for her.

Gale stirred. Cedar scrambled backward, acting as if she were guilty of something. Maybe she was. She had been admiring his body while he was passed out in bed. She only came in here to wake the polar bear up. She cursed herself for getting distracted. If she was going to survive living with Gale, living in Eurio, she really did need to control herself better.

"Good morning, Sunshine," Cedar said as she

looked over to Gale's window. She drew back the curtains, allowing in the scarce Sunlight.

"Don't try to access Solsis again without me here," she instructed. "You don't want to accidentally burn down the town."

When she looked back at Gale, he was snoring. Sunlight was shining in his eyes, and he didn't give a damn. Apparently, he wasn't going to wake up easily.

She moved back over to his bedside and placed her hand on his shoulder. She ignored the hard and warm feel of him underneath her palm and fingers. She ignored the needy pulses in her sex. She shook him. "Up and at 'em!" she shouted.

Gale grabbed her waist. Cedar hadn't expected it, and she toppled over on him. Suddenly, she was straddling him, almost perfectly aligned. She was sitting directly on his hips. But his eyes were still closed. His fingers were like iron as she tried to struggle out of his grip. He had big hands. Her waist was wide, but his hands were so big, she figured they could wrap all the way around the waist of one of those skinny girls. Nevertheless, he had her in quite a hold. And struggling made things worse. What was he? A boa constrictor? She rolled her hips with the intention of getting away, but his hard-on hit just right in between her legs. He was getting harder by the second. She wanted that blanket between them gone so she could see everything. Her mouth watered at the thought, as if she were anticipating eating a big, juicy steak.

She took in a shuddering breath and stopped moving. She grabbed his wrists and tried to pull him off of her. When that didn't work, she tried prying his fingers loose one by one. Nothing worked. His eyes were closed, and he was breathing deeply.

"Gale," she said, exasperated. "Are you awake, or is this your variation of sleepwalking?"

He didn't say anything, but she saw his nostrils flare and noticed a change in the rhythm of his breathing. At the very least, she was certain she was starting to rouse him. She wasn't sure what else to do, so she reached out for his face. His chin and cheeks were smooth, though she found some stray hairs he needed to shave. It seemed his clan, much like hers, didn't have the gene for thick body hair. She smiled at that. His skin felt good, warm. She marveled at the edges of his face. They were so sharp, she was certain she could use his chin as a knife. And yet, he also had a roundness to his features. God, and he was big. So big.

Gale opened his eyes. They were a medium

brown, flat at a glance, but the light gave them an un-fathomable depth; Cedar could easily get lost in them. After clearing her throat, she placed her hands back on Gale's wrists. "Good. You're awake," she said. "Mind letting me go now?"

Gale growled. "I do mind."

Cedar froze. Her fingers grew slack against his wrists. "Gale—"

"You feel good."

She rolled her eyes. "I know you had a lot to drink last night. I also know *Solsis* can be intoxicating. It's like fire in the senses. It's a little unpredictable too. What you're feeling is its residual power."

She wasn't making that up. His current arousal could have been because of the leftover tingles Solsis left in his body. She might have written her own arousal off as the same thing, but she had been feeling this way about Gale since she first met him, so she wasn't going to blame it on something else. It was all her. And she had it bad. She was wet, so wet she could feel it coming through her pants. She wanted to move, to rock against his hard-on, because he was *very* hard underneath her now. He felt huge.

Gale's nostrils flared. "I smell your need."

Cedar nearly lost her mind when he bucked up. He

hit her just right again, through her clothes and the blanket barrier. Her hands left his wrists and instinctively went to his chest. She dug her fingers into his skin and arched her back. Her breathing was suddenly heavy. She dug into his skin a little harder, biting down with her nails. "No," she said. "I am not having sex with you unless you're sober."

"You'll have sex with me if I'm sober?" he asked. His pupils were dilated, hungry. "What do I have to do to prove it?"

Cedar's head was spinning. "I don't know. There isn't a test for residual Solsis, but you don't have a hangover from last night, and you definitely should."

Gale chuckled. "You're so wet."

Cedar's cheeks grew hot. She shimmied uncomfortably, though Gale continued to hold her in place. "I can't help it," she squeaked.

"What is it about me you like so much?" he asked.

"I wonder the same thing." She cleared her throat. "Other than your perfect face and sexy body of course. Because you totally have a perfect face and a sexy body. And I've seen you naked many times for having only known you a day."

"Such animals," Gale said. He experimented with another little buck of his hips. Cedar whimpered. She wanted to bury her nails into his skin, but that would risk drawing blood, and she didn't want to do that. Did she? She didn't even understand what was going on right now.

She babbled, nearly incoherent. "Shifters find mates differently from humans. Sense of smell for most of us is very telling, and nudity isn't weird, and neither is mating when you've only known that shifter a day."

Gale laughed a bit louder this time. "I think *you* might be drunk, Cedar."

"All right, I give," she said. Her resolve faded. If he wanted to have sex with her, if he was sober and meant it—which it certainly seemed like he did—she wasn't going to say no. Sex didn't have to turn into anything permanent. She liked sex as much as anyone. "But this is a one-time deal."

"Am I sober then? Do I pass?" Gale asked.

"I guess you do."

He released her waist, but it was just so he could roll up the edges of her sweater, touch her skin, and gently grab her love handles.

"Take it off," he said.

Cedar pulled her sweater over her head and shook out her disheveled hair once the deed was done. Gale sat up, moving her down onto his lap as he wrapped his big arms around her. It took him a moment to navigate through her long hair, but he found the back of her bra. Cedar liked that he was big enough to hold her like this and make her feel tiny. She didn't want to be tiny, but she liked feeling his power. She liked that he was much bigger than her.

Gale discarded her bra to the floor. He pressed his chest against hers, and she melted against him. Her nipples were hard, sensitive points. His skin on hers was almost enough to make her come. She had never been this thirsty in her life. She didn't want to think about it, but she knew she was getting well past mating years as far as shifters were concerned. This was all likely the result of her polar bear demanding a mate. But Cedar didn't want a mate. She had already made that decision. Kind of…

Gale kissed her, his lips on her jaw. She clung to his back and dug her nails deeper into his skin until his lips met hers. He tasted like that cheap booze he drank last night. It might have offended her particular palate if she hadn't been so hungry for him. Because she could taste him through it, like a drug, and she needed more. She let his tongue into her mouth without making him work for it. She let him explore before gently nibbling at him. Then he let her take the lead. The smacking sounds of their lips connecting and disconnecting raised the hairs on the back of her neck.

She had it bad.

Gale kneaded her flesh, never settling on one place. It was like he needed to feel every inch of her.

And it made her think.

Cedar didn't want to be one of those skinny girls, but that didn't mean others didn't judge her for her weight. The last guy she slept with told her to lose weight after they were done, after he got off and she thought everything was going so well. She got angry just thinking about it. She hadn't slept with anyone in a long time because of it.

Gale stopped kissing her. "Change your mind?"

Cedar pushed the thoughts away and kissed him again. The last thing she wanted was for him to disengage. "It's nothing. Just thinking about some jerk I slept with months ago."

"You aren't exclusive with anyone, are you? I have to know," Gale said. He moved away from her kisses and searched her eyes.

"No. I'm unattached," she said.

"Good." Gale's chest rumbled against hers, and Cedar tried to squeeze her thighs together, but Gale was in the way.

"Why's that good?" she asked.

"I wouldn't want to make a potential mate jealous. Not into stealing other men's girls."

"What kind of girl do you think I am?" Cedar remarked.

"A temptress. Never jumped in bed with anyone so fast. Never even thought to."

Cedar didn't get the chance to add to that thought. Gale moved underneath her, flipped her over so she was the one with her back against the bed. Gale held himself up, hands and legs spread at her sides. He kissed the middle of her chest, in between her breasts, and nibbled on her skin. He moved back to work on her pants. He carefully tugged them off her legs and went for her underwear. He was less careful about that, and Cedar heard the elastic band protest. She felt it too.

"Hey, don't break my clothes," she warned. "I don't have much here." Then she saw something new, something she hadn't noticed when she had seen him naked before. It was a faded scar on his left bicep, and it was the result of a hard bite. She knew what it was, but she asked anyway. "What's that bite?"

Gale growled. He bit her hip, and she jolted, forgetting her question. She tried to see underneath him, curious about how hard he was, about how big he was with all that blood rushing to his cock. But Gale didn't give her a chance to look. He was as close to her as he could be without being inside of her. He tweaked one of her nipples. She yelped and then moaned as he drew the hard point into his mouth and sucked. Cedar's hands had a mind of their own, digging into Gale's back, ripping skin as her nails trailed down to his hips. She tried to grab his cock, but he drew back. Cedar huffed her frustration.

"I'm trying to go down on you, woman," Gale said. "Are you going to let me do that or not?"

Cedar couldn't remember anyone ever going down on her before. That was because no one ever had. She hadn't been lucky enough to find such a giving partner. Then again, she never usually slept with anyone more than once.

Her inner thighs were slick with her arousal, and her pussy clenched again with the thought of Gale's lips teasing her now.

"Okay," Cedar said. "You're in charge here."

"Thank you," Gale said. He bit her nipple hard enough to hurt, but not hard enough to escape that pleasure-pain threshold. He licked her afterward, and her stomach did a weird jump. He traced her skin with his tongue, lips, and teeth until he made it down to the space between her thighs. She spread her legs as far as she could to give him better access. Gale wasted no time diving into her wet folds with his tongue. Cedar moaned. Every time Gale licked her, the pulsing intensified. He introduced his teeth next, nibbling her clit.

"You smell so good," he said with a rumble. She heard each time he took in a big whiff of her scent. Her heart beat unevenly inside of her chest. Then he licked her again and slid two fingers inside of her. She was so wet, there was no resistance. He worked her like that while he somehow crumpled into this little ball. She was whimpering his name deliriously now, begging for more.

He took his tongue and lips away and grabbed her thighs, angling her body so he could pump into her better. It became a merciless rhythm that never tired, an onslaught. He introduced three fingers, and Cedar's body twinged. It hurt for just a moment before she came violently around his fingers, her entire body crashing with the force of her orgasm. He kept going and applied pressure on her sensitive clit with his thumb. He nearly had her jumping out of her skin as he made her come again. It was too much. Her head was so fuzzy, she couldn't think. But she forced herself to when Gale moved like he was finally getting ready to use that lethal sword of his.

"Wait," she said, suddenly very alert. She should have asked this before they got this far. Hell, where was her mind at? "We're not doing that unless you have a condom."

"Okay," Gale said easily. "But we are doing it if I do have a condom?"

At least he was considerate. He wasn't like other men Cedar had slept with. He made sure that she was okay with every step he took. She appreciated that. It was the minimum requirement for banging someone, but so many people seemed to forget that. Lucky for her, she was a polar-bear shifter. Not many could push her around, so she had never run into any problems herself.

"I know it's supposed to feel better without one or whatever but safety first, and I'm not on birth control anymore because it didn't really agree with my body. I haven't been with anybody for months anyway," Cedar explained. Female shifters were lucky human birth control seemed to work for them at all. She knew it worked pretty much perfectly for some female shifters, but everyone was different. There were also plenty of female shifters who wouldn't even try it because they were so doctor shy. Doctors were usually fine if blood wasn't involved—and there were a fair number of shifters among doctors themselves; they were a big part of why shifters hadn't been outed to humans.

Cedar sat up when Gale got off the bed. He walked over to a drawer and retrieved an untouched condom. "Seems I have to thank Weston for keeping me stocked after all," he remarked.

When Gale didn't expand on that, Cedar raised an eyebrow. She thought about asking him to offer up more information, but she didn't. Maybe Gale hadn't done this in a while, maybe not since his mate died, and Weston kept him "stocked" up on condoms because he hoped Gale would move on someday.

Cedar didn't want to think about that.

Instead, she took the opportunity of him standing to *look* at him. She finally got the chance to stare at his thick length. He was *huge*, like, bigger than she had imagined he'd be when very, very hard. She watched with great interest as he made to put on the condom. She was especially interested in the silky red tip of his cock. The foreskin was rolled back, and he was dripping precum. When he was done with the condom, he held his dick up and dropped it, fully aware she was watching. His cock bounced just slightly, holding firm, determined to do its duty. Cedar didn't think she could get any wetter, but she was so very wrong.

"Ready for me?" Gale asked, his nostrils flaring. Cedar knew he knew the answer, but he kept up with his asking routine.

"I am very ready for you, sexy polar bear." She spread her legs wider, pressed down onto the balls of her feet, and beckoned him back onto the bed. He did as she asked, crawling over her and wedging himself between her legs. He eased his hips down to hers and tested the positioning. He barely breached her ready body with the head of his cock, teasing.

"You didn't even ask if your son was here," Cedar commented.

"He's at school. You took him this morning. I heard."

"You were awake this morning?"

"Barely. Needed to sleep the rest of that booze off and that tingling from the Sun Magic. It's still kind of there, though. The tingling."

"Solsis can do that to you. The power's addicting, huh? I figure that's why you want sex so badly right now." She felt his arms, moving her hands down each muscle and confirming he was just as hard as he looked while enjoying the softness of his skin. She found that faded bite mark again, but this time she didn't try to ask about it.

"Maybe," Gale said. "Thank you, by the way. For taking Ike to school."

"No problem. He's a good cub."

Gale thrust, burying himself farther inside of her, but he wasn't deep enough just yet.

"I never wanted cubs," Cedar said, running her mouth like she did sometimes. "But if I knew they'd end up like Ike, maybe I'd change my mind." She let out an *oof!* when Gale thrust again, burying himself as far as he could go. No one had ever filled her up so perfectly. Then again, she had never had sex with another bear shifter. The whole not-wanting-a-mate thing and all. It was a real shame, though. Gale was a perfect fit.

"So that's why you're not mated," Gale said. He experimented by rolling his hips. It must have felt as good for him as it did her because his eyes threatened to roll back. He let out a pleasure-filled grunt.

"That and I'm not exactly most people's first pick," Cedar added. Then she cursed herself for saying it. It didn't matter what other people thought. She didn't care. She liked herself the way she was.

"I find that hard to believe," Gale said as he thrust again.

The tension was ratcheting up. Cedar wasn't sure

how much longer she would be able to carry a conversation. She was getting ready to climax again. Gale made sex extremely good. If having a mate, a bear mate, meant multiple orgasms every time they had sex, maybe she should consider finding herself one. Maybe. It wasn't that she had anything against mates. She liked the idea of someone by her side, on her side, no matter what. She wanted a mate to be devoted to her, and she didn't want to be a breeding machine, a means for a male to pass on his genes.

Gale picked up the pace and found a perfect rhythm. Cedar pressed upward, clung to him, and begged him to keep going because she was so close.

"Almost there!" she screamed. "More!"

Gale growled and shouted, "*Iris!*"

Cedar froze.

The high she was feeling collapsed alongside her mental state. She couldn't do anything about all the stimulation her body was experiencing, so she still came—spectacularly—when he came too. But it was short-lived.

She had enough.

She pushed at his iron chest, doing her best to ignore his pulsing dick, the perfect fit.

"Get off of me!" she growled.

Gale pulled out with great haste. "Cedar, I—"

"Not a word."

"Cedar—"

"Shut up!" Cedar shrieked. She sat up and slapped Gale across the cheek. Her hand stung. His face was red. Tears streamed out of her eyes. "I don't even look like her! I have a similar hair color and skin tone. Our clans might be related generations back, but she's not me. We don't have the same face. I'm not just a body to fill the void, Gale! You were with Iris this whole time." She breathed in an ugly sniffle. Her nose was running now too. Great.

"This was a one-time thing. That's what I said, but I wanted you to be with *me*. Just for the moment. No strings attached. No expectations." She wiped at her eyes. She pushed him again, making sure he wasn't anywhere near her. "That's it. I'm done being second best. Sex could be nice, but not when guys keep telling me I'm fat and need to lose weight or when they call me by the name of their dead mate!"

She got off the bed and made a grab for her clothes. She wanted to shower, to wash away his scent all over her body, but she didn't have time. She needed out of this cabin. She needed to get away from him.

"Cedar!" Gale called.

She didn't wait. She ran. She grabbed her boots, put them on in record time, and then went for her coat. Gale followed her to the front door. He had pants now. Was he going to stop her?

Her heart hammered inside of her chest as she burst out the door, not bothering to close it. She ran without a destination in the snow and empty cold. It was hard to see through her burning eyes, but she wasn't going back. If Gale knew what was good for him, he wouldn't follow her. She would tear him to shreds. Her bear was angry, enraged like she never had been before.

Cedar slowed her pace after a few minutes. She doubled over, hands resting on her thighs. She took a moment to remind herself how to breathe, and then she kept going. She reminded herself that she was amazing, valid, beautiful, allowed to be anything she wanted to be, that it didn't matter what men said to her. It didn't matter that everyone in her clan found their place with mates, happy to settle and breed. She had been through this self-doubt before. She didn't regret her decision not to settle back home.

But sometimes being different was painful. Being so far away from a family she loved, being estranged, was painful. Doubt stayed.

And she almost wondered if there was something wrong with her.

CHAPTER 11

CEDAR WALKED ALONE IN the snow, still
sniffling. She didn't know where she was going,
just that she was going. *Stupid Gale,* she thought. She
didn't know if she wanted to go back to his cabin at all.
She knew she didn't really have a choice, though; she
left her things back there. But seriously, what was that
all about? Gale was so lost in his deceased mate that he
couldn't even enjoy a moment with her? How long had
it been since Iris died? Six years? Cedar wasn't trying
to be insensitive, but Gale said Iris's name when he was
inside of Cedar. The thought made her want to puke. It
was all wrong.

Cedar sniffled again. Her sensitive ears caught

voices nearby. She looked over her shoulder to see Ike, Austin, Mateo, even the Lenkovs, with all of Austin's students, trudging through the snow. They were all bundled up, and most of them were carrying or pulling sleds.

"Cedar!" Ike exclaimed. He ran up to her, pulling a rope attached to a sled behind him. "What are you doing here?" he asked. "Did you and Weston talk this long?"

"No. Just out for a walk." Cedar hoped her eyes weren't as red and puffy as they felt. It felt like there were little grains of sand underneath her eyelids every time she blinked. "What are you all doing?"

"We're going sledding for a change of pace," Austin replied. "Want to join us?"

"Sure." Cedar shrugged.

"Mateo and those two know the best mountain apparently." Austin nodded toward the Lenkovs and sighed. "Hopefully it's not too dangerous."

Mateo clapped his mate's shoulder. "It's fine."

"Your definition of fine and my definition of fine don't always line up."

"Austin, you worry too much." Mateo kissed his cheek. "You trust me, right?"

"With my life, but I don't know about the tigers."

"Hey," Lance said. But his tone was flat.

Austin looked over his shoulder to smile at the tigers, but it seemed half-hearted.

"Austin." Mateo's voice was quiet.

"It's going to be fun!" Austin said. "This is what you all voted for. Right, class?"

The kids cheered, but they hid safely behind Austin and the other adult shifters they trusted. They peeked out from behind them at times to stare at Ike next to Cedar, though.

Yuri's gaze drifted to Cedar. Lance's gaze followed; it was no warmer than the last time he had laid eyes on her.

"Well, lead the way," Cedar said. She had been invited, and icy glares didn't scare her.

Ike gave her a warm smile that fought off the chills anyway and said, "You'll have fun, Cedar. I promise. You can ride on my sled with me."

Why was this kid so cute?

He took her hand with his free one as he continued to pull his sled behind him with the other. Cedar didn't know if the kid could see that she needed comfort or if he was warm like this naturally, but she was getting pretty envious about him being Gale's kid instead of hers.

She never disliked kids or anything, but she never wanted them either, because she didn't want to be a breeder. She wanted to go out into the world, be her own woman. In her clan, females were expected to stay home and raise the cubs. When she left, she was relieved to find there were more options than that for her. That didn't mean she was against having her own family someday.

With the cub's hand in hers, Cedar followed the others through the new snow and the spruces, passing the occasional cabin along the way. Eventually, they hit an incline that kept going up and up and up. She felt it in her burning legs. She hadn't realized how much sitting she had done since leaving her clan. Office work didn't require a lot of moving around. She was out of shape. She was glad her fishing skills, although rusty, held up so well despite that. It was likely her competitive side was what made up for it, though, because she hadn't done anything like that in years. She was a domestic polar bear now. And she hadn't had simple "fun" in a long time. She couldn't remember the last time she went sledding.

Cedar almost slipped in the snow thanks to her protesting legs, but Ike caught her. He was surprisingly strong for his size. He was big for his age, but still, she was impressed.

"Watch your step," he said with a grin.

"Thank you, Ike. I feel better knowing I have you looking out for me."

His grin grew wider.

"Ike has a crush!" a girl squawked. She smelled like some type of bird. Cedar recognized her from when Gale took her and Bruiser to the school. She didn't know her name, though. The information she had on the students was some of the sketchiest, likely because many of them were among the newest arrivals.

Cedar thought Ike might make a comeback, like kids did, deny it at least, but he didn't. He stuck close to Cedar, ignoring the jab entirely. He held her hand without a care; the words fell like water off his back.

"You're wasting your time, Janice," one of the other students whispered. Cedar recognized this one, too. His scent was distinctly wolf. "You'll never get under his skin." His eyes were practically sparkling as he said the words.

Clearly, Cedar thought. Ike was much more level-headed than she was at seven. She noticed the young wolf shifter carefully eyeing Ike. When Ike looked his way, the wolf flashed a hesitant smile before returning his gaze to the snow below.

"Who's that?" Cedar whispered.

"Neil. He's new," Ike replied.

"You friends?"

Ike shrugged. "Not really."

"I think he'd like to be friends."

Ike looked at Neil again, and this time Neil gave a shy wave. Ike returned the gesture with an added boost of confidence. *To be young,* Cedar thought. Relationships were easier then—not like the shit that just went down with Gale. She pressed her lips together until they were drained of color. Then she let it go. For now.

They had made it to the top of the mountain. Cedar was really feeling the burn now, mainly in her calves. She huffed a few breaths of hot air, condensation thick in front of her eyes. She exhaled slowly to even out the heat suffocating her system and observed her place on top of the world. The way they had come up was full of spruces, but this side of the mountain was almost entirely white. It would be smooth sailing all the way down to the bottom.

"See?" Mateo said, squeezing Austin's shoulder. "The best mountain for sledding."

"This side of it anyway," Cedar commented and shielded her eyes to see better. "Except for some huge rocks."

"For jumps," Lance said. "The perfect mountain." He signed something to his brother.

Yuri asked, "Ready?"

Lance nodded, signing again as he spoke. "See you slowpokes at the bottom."

"Beat you to it," Mateo called. He and Austin were somehow sitting on the same rather small sled. Austin was seated in front, and Mateo was behind him. Mateo eagerly wrapped his arms around his mate's waist and was about to push off.

"Wait!" Austin said. "Why am *I* in the front?"

"You're steering, babe," Mateo said. Then he pushed off, propelling them down the mountain. Austin let out a short, terrified shriek before taking the reins. They swerved every which way and Mateo shouted for Austin to take the jump. Austin did as his mate asked, and then the two of them were flying in the air. This time Austin was full-on screaming. Mateo laughed as he held both his mate and the sled in his hands. They landed without crashing, and their laughter echoed all the way back up the mountain.

"Those two are disgusting," Lance said and petulantly stuck out his tongue.

A couple students shot off down the mountain next, weaving back and forth and creating their own

CHRISTMAS POLAR BEAR

trails. Some of them veered toward the rocks, taking jumps, while others stayed on a safe course. The growing laughter was contagious.

"I think they're sweet," Cedar said, spying Austin and Mateo stopped at the mountain's base. They were rolling around in the snow now.

"Women," Lance said. "Romantics, all of them."

"What's that supposed to mean? Are you trying to start a fight?"

"I'm stating a fact." His lip curled up, displaying teeth. Maybe his intention wasn't to start a fight, but he wouldn't mind one.

Yuri stood in front of Lance, hands up, likely in reaction to Cedar's growling. At first, she thought he was doing it to cut through the sudden static in the air, but he was grinning like a lunatic and only added to it.

"Whatever Lance said, he didn't mean it," Yuri said and slung his arm around the back of Lance's neck. He pulled Lance down to rub his knuckles over the top of Lance's head, causing short white-blond hairs to stick up in odd places as Lance struggled to get free.

Wasn't Yuri bedridden just yesterday? Cedar shrugged it off.

"Ike, we're racing those two to the bottom of the mountain," she announced.

"Okay," Ike said easily. He planted his sled in the snow and shuffled from one foot to the other as he bounced up and down.

When Lance got free, he signed something to his brother. Yuri grinned. The way that smile lit up his face, the way he was exuding energy, almost hid the fatigue he must have felt down to his bones. Almost. The dark circles under his eyes were still there.

Cedar sat down first. It took a little bit of effort to find a way to sit snuggly on the sled while providing a space for Ike. Lance and Yuri lined up their separate sleds with Ike and Cedar's and sat down too.

"Just growl or something to signal when to go," Yuri said. His eyes were trained on some unseen point ahead like he was getting ready to pounce on unsuspecting prey.

Lance placed his hand on Yuri's shoulder to get his attention. He signed and said, "Janice will whistle. That's the signal."

"Got it."

"You've got to steer us to victory." Cedar patted Ike on the shoulder.

"I will," Ike replied, hunkering down in front of her.

Cedar settled for holding the sides of the sled to

keep them steady while giving Ike room to breathe. "Just tell me what to do. Lean left, lean right, whatever you need," Cedar said.

"Okay," Ike replied.

"You two are going down," Lance informed. He didn't look at Ike. He stared at Cedar with cold blue eyes that coaxed a shiver down her spine; it felt like he had just poured ice water down her back.

Janice whistled loud and clear, and Cedar pushed off with all her might. Her heart beat loudly in her chest as she and Ike narrowly took the lead. Ike lowered himself against the sled for better aerodynamics, and Cedar followed suit. She tried to ignore anything else as she focused on their destination and on Ike. She followed his movements and kept her ears sharp for any instructions he might throw her way. The little guy steered clear of the jumps but otherwise kept them on a straight line to the bottom. They picked up speed until they got caught on a trail that had been taken by several other sledders.

"Lean left!" Ike shouted.

Cedar did what he asked, but they were too late. They ended up hitting a rock not quite head-on and spiraled into the air. Cedar landed on her back, and Ike landed on top of her somehow. She instinctively wrapped her arms around him as they both slid down the mountain with Cedar as their new sled. They picked up speed well and still made it to the bottom of the mountain. The two of them were caught in a fit of giggles when they finally stopped. They were laughing so hard, Ike was doubled-over on Cedar, unable to move.

"Did we win?" Cedar asked, out of breath. She released her arms to her sides, and Ike rolled off of her.

"I don't know. I couldn't see," the cub said. He wiped a few icy happy tears from his eyes as he grinned.

Ike got to his feet and proceeded to help Cedar to hers. They looked around until they spied the Lenkovs farther away. Their sleds were shoved to the side, and Lance was hunched over Yuri, who was crumpled in the snow. Mateo and Austin scurried over after Austin told his students to stay back.

"Something's wrong," Cedar said.

She and Ike pressed forward to see Yuri convulsing in the snow. Lance quickly moved in front of the only rock nearby to act as a much softer cushion should Yuri come his way. Lance's face scrunched up, and he bit his lower lip as he watched his brother helplessly struggle.

"What should we do?" Cedar asked. "He's having a

seizure."

"Wait it out," Mateo growled. His fists clenched, and his eyes burned yellow. A vein throbbed in his neck as his jaw clenched.

"That's it? That's all we can do?"

"There is nothing else!" Every muscle in Mateo's body was tense. The wolf was going to rip out at any moment.

Austin took Mateo's face in his hands and coaxed him down until their noses touched. "Focus on me. Okay, Mateo? It's going to be okay."

Mateo was panting, plagued by shallow breaths. He did his best to do what his mate asked, but his eyes refused to focus; the yellow wanted to stay.

"Bring Mateo over here." Cedar led them away from the Lenkovs and those surrounding. Ike followed her as well.

"Don't look back," Austin said when Mateo was about to look over his shoulder.

"I don't know what to do," Mateo muttered through labored breaths.

"Staying calm would be helpful," Cedar said. "I need you to answer some questions, Mateo. It could help Yuri."

Mateo blinked the yellow away. "How?"

"Depending on the situation, I can call in a White Witch. A White Witch might be able to help Yuri in a way that doctors can't."

A storm clouded Mateo's face. The yellow in his eyes flashed like lightning waiting to strike. "Eurio doesn't like witches." Then he cocked his head. "Witches can use magic to heal?"

Cedar frowned. "Yes, White Magic. Trinity has some very excellent witches who could—"

"No!" Lance was on his feet, eyes locked onto Cedar. The icy blue in his eyes flashed red, and a snarl took his lips. He could have been Mateo's twin.

"It seems Eurio isn't well informed about witches at all. Is that why Yuri won't see one, because you've only heard bad things?" Cedar pressed.

Lance's eyes dropped to the snow.

"You won't let him see one."

He snarled.

Mateo intervened. "Lance, I think we can trust Cedar—"

"No," Lance growled low in his throat. He caught hold of his convulsing brother, wrangling him like a flailing fish flicking snow every which way, and picked him up.

"I don't think that's a good idea!" Cedar exclaimed.

She held out her hands as if the gesture alone could get Lance to back down.

"No witches," Lance said. It was impressive he was able to hold on to his brother at all with the way he was thrashing. One of his berserk hands jerked up and scratched Lance along his jaw. It was a rather deep cut that oozed blood as soon as it was made.

Cedar held up her hands, reeling them back toward her person, placating. "Set him down, Lance. This isn't safe for either of you." She hadn't had any firsthand experience with seizures herself, but she had eyes.

Mateo growled. "What's going on? I thought you wanted to help Yuri. I thought you'd do anything."

"You don't know a thing about witches, Mateo." Lance held his brother firmly in his arms and took heavy steps in the snow, slowly dragging both of their bodies away.

"No, I don't. Everyone here says they're bad news, and I've listened, but they can't be all bad if Trinity works with them! We're allied with Trinity. We wouldn't be if they were bad shifters. Gale wouldn't allow that. What if a witch could help Yuri? I didn't even know this was an option!"

"*Cedar* says to bring in a witch and you're gung-ho? We don't even know her!"

"Lance, Yuri's been getting so bad, and he keeps getting worse. I know he hates doctors and shit too, but this is too much."

Yuri jerked, and Lance wasn't ready for him. He fell to his knees but held his brother close. He was especially protective of Yuri's head, cradling it like an infant's; right now, he was just as fragile as one. Mateo rushed over, but Lance roared at him. "Stay away! All of you, stay away."

Mateo whimpered, a sound more wolf than man. Lance pulled his brother up to his side. He managed it without much trouble because only small trembles racked Yuri's body now. It looked like he might be coming out of the seizure.

"L-Lance." Yuri grimaced as he tried to grasp his brother's coat with shaking fingers.

"I've got you, Yuri. We're going home." Lance highlighted his words by rubbing his cheek against his brother's. Yuri couldn't understand his words, but the simple touch was the reassurance he needed. He steadied as well as he was able to.

"Lance!" Mateo called again.

But Lance didn't budge. He wasn't listening anymore. He dragged his brother away without another word and left the rest of them standing there, dumb-founded. Quiet.

Cedar folded her arms as Ike fidgeted at her side. He looked up at her, back down at his feet, and then he grabbed her coat. She gave him a one-armed hug. And she decided. She was going to call in a White Witch anyway. She wouldn't tell anyone. Eurio's shifters might be furious with her, but if a White Witch could help, it would be worth incurring their wrath.

CHAPTER 12

"THEY SHOULD BE HOME soon, Gale. Go and apologize for whatever you did, because you're not hiding your feelings well at all," Cary said.

Gale did not know what to say to that. He was distressed. He had royally fucked up.

"Cedar's something, isn't she?" he asked. He looked at the organized files on the table. Apparently, the she-bear had come over here earlier to get some work done. She discussed some things with Weston, and then she proceeded to organize files. She digitized a bunch of it onto her laptop too, no doubt ready to send it off to Trinity at any moment. She worked amazingly fast.

"Yes, she's certainly efficient," Weston said. "She's also nosy in an I-care-about-you kind of way. And she's quite a beauty."

Cary didn't correct her mate, and Gale knew why. Weston said it for Gale. Because of Gale.

"What do you really think of her?" Gale asked.

"Exactly what I said. If you like her, catch her."

Gale's stomach twisted itself into knots. Oh, he did like her. More than he was comfortable with. Just over a day, she had managed to captivate him, and it was all because Trinity had assigned her to Eurio. There wasn't an instant spark or anything like that, not for him. She and Ike hit it off right away, but if he hadn't been forced to spend so much time with her, he would have promptly done his best to forget about her like he did anyone who showed a remote amount of interest in him—and Cedar was interested. But each passing moment he was forced to spend with her made her that much more intriguing. She carried herself with confidence, she had a sunny smile, and her fishing skills were ridiculous. She was nosy like Weston said but in the most genuine way possible.

He had acted hastily when traces of Solsis continued to buzz in his veins after his first encounter with it last night. He was sober now, and while he did not in any way regret having sex with Cedar, it happened too soon. He had way too much baggage, and he hurt her because of it.

"Thanks for your time," Gale said.

"No problem." Weston escorted him to the door. "You better listen to my mate. It's better to apologize for anything you do wrong right away." He frowned. "Do I even want to know what you did? Do you want to talk about it?"

"We're old friends, Weston, but we've never *talked*."

"Yeah, my mate gets real pissy about that sometimes."

"Weston," Cary chided from the hall.

Gale chuckled. "I fucked up, and now I have to make things right. That's all there is to it."

Weston nodded. "Good luck."

The wolf shifter was over a decade older than Gale, but friendship wasn't restricted by age. Weston felt like a brother in many ways. And yet he, like everyone else, often felt like a stranger these days. Gale didn't know how to let people in anymore. He had good relationships, he had friends, but he was distant. It was worst with Ike. Mateo knew that better than anyone, and yet he still thought Gale was good. Gale thought it was a good thing Ike had that out-of-control wolf shifter for a brother, because he loved and showed love much better than Gale did.

Gale pulled the collar of his coat snugly around his neck as a cold breeze whistled by him. He listened to the sound of his boots as they sunk into the snow, and his stomach twisted tighter. He felt awful about what he did to Cedar. He wanted to go back in time and banish Iris from his mind. She wasn't supposed to be there with him in that moment. He wanted to have sex with *Cedar.* He wanted to be with *her.*

He just didn't know how to let go.

For some reason, deep down inside, he had felt as if he were *cheating* on his *deceased* mate—especially after Cedar had spotted his scar. Iris's scar. It brought up thoughts of her, put her name on his lips. But she was with the spirits. She was one of the many lights that made up the auroras that graced the sky at times. She had ascended and left this world behind. So why?

Had he done something wrong? Did she look down on him from time to time and was she disappointed?

His brain went fuzzy like radio static, and he couldn't think about it anymore. It wasn't as if he truly believed those old stories about spirits anyway. They were tales he was told as a child. At the age of thirty-two, he had seen much more of the world than Eurio. He had learned about way too many theories, religions, sciences, and facts to believe such a simple, mystical explanation now; the old clan stories had nothing to back them up.

Life had been simpler before Iris left to see the world and he followed in her footsteps.

Gale returned to his cabin, stripped off all his warm winter gear, and paced as he tried to figure out a way to apologize. It couldn't be as easy as saying he was sorry. Nope. That wouldn't cut it. The cabin was quiet, and he was alone, but he doubted that would last for much longer; school was out. Blame the pressure of time or something else, but he couldn't come up with anything. He had no idea how to apologize for what he did. No apology would fix it. All he could do was tell Cedar the truth. It wouldn't be about asking forgiveness. He probably didn't deserve it anyway, but Cedar needed to know that what happened was not because of her. It was his own problem. She had taken a blow to her self-esteem, and that was unacceptable. He would build her back up and bolster her confidence. He couldn't let her radiant light dim because of him.

Familiar voices caught Gale's attention. He sucked

in a big breath as the front door opened. Cedar took one look at him and then quickly looked away. Ike did the exact same thing. However, Cedar stayed standing at the door after she closed it while Ike ducked his head and walked past Gale for his room without saying a word. A whimper tried to fight its way out of Gale's mouth, but he pressed his lips together tightly. He let the awful feeling wash over him in cold, relentless waves because he deserved it. How many times had he done the same thing to his cub?

Cedar folded her arms. When Gale didn't move, she beckoned him with a wiggling finger. Hesitantly, he did as she asked. He wondered why she wanted him closer. He wondered if she intended on slapping him again. He wasn't looking forward to that if she was. His face had been red for a good thirty minutes after she stormed out of the house.

Cedar kept her voice low as she said, "You need to spend more time with Ike. By more, I mean *actually* spend time with him. Your relationship is just passing a couple words here and there, isn't it? I've spent more time with him since I've been here than you probably have in a month."

Gale cringed. She was close enough. "I know. I… I know."

"You're not trying hard enough. You care about your cub, Gale. I can see it. Everyone can see it. There's something stopping you from really connecting to him. Is it Iris?"

This Trinity Shifter could see right through him.

"I'm sorry, Cedar," Gale said. "I fucking messed up. I wasn't even thinking about Iris until—"

"Until you climaxed." There was a growl in her throat, though she was doing her best to keep it quiet.

"It's not what you think," Gale insisted. He glanced at Ike's door. He didn't want to have this conversation right outside of his cub's room. "Can we talk outside?"

Cedar opened the door again, holding out her hand for Gale to lead the way. He grabbed his coat and did just that. They didn't walk far, just to the neighboring white and black spruces. Gale leaned back against one of the trunks.

"Iris and I kind of had a fucked-up relationship," he said.

"I've heard all about Iris," Cedar replied. "She was a handful."

"Will you hear my side of everything?"

Snowflakes fell from the sky as if in response to Cedar's silence. And Gale waited. He was patient.

"Yes, I'll hear it from you," she said at last.

Gale looked up at the tree branches above him to gather his thoughts. The snow weighed them down. It would either give way by sliding off the branches when it got too heavy, or those branches would snap. He wondered which would prevail. The sky was darkening more and more by the second. Soon the moon and stars were the only light source aside from the lights on inside of the cabin.

"I loved Iris my entire life," Gale began. "We grew up together in Eurio as part of the Loike Clan. I had it set in my mind since I was a young cub that we would be mates. I told her that same thing one day when we were five. She said okay. But, you know, we were young. Kids say things they don't understand. But I meant it, even though I didn't really understand everything about mates."

"Not all bears believe in mates anyway," Cedar commented. "It's not actually in our nature, you know?"

"You're right. We must have gotten it from the Toran Pack. Those wolves have been our neighbors forever."

"No idea where my clan got it from," she grumbled.

Gale smiled at that. "You don't like the idea of a

monogamous relationship, Cedar?"

She shrugged. "I didn't say *that*. But my clan was obsessed with females staying home to raise cubs when I was the best fisher there!"

Gale glanced at her, gaze soft. She stared at the cabin and puffed out hot breaths into the cold. Red dusted her cheeks. "You are an excellent fisher," he agreed. "And that's not all. Trinity obviously values your skills."

She nodded one too many times.

"Raising cubs is an important job too," Gale added. "Iris wasn't good at it. She didn't have the patience for it. She left me in charge of Ike most of the time, and that was fine because we fit like that, until she died."

"I didn't mean…" Cedar's voice trailed off.

"It's good you left your clan. You have the right to choose who you are, who you want to be, and what you want to do. Gender roles be damned, right?"

She pursed her lips. But she *looked* at him. For the first time since coming back, she looked at him without a sharpness in her brown eyes. He could see inside of them like they were clear pools of water. He could see *her*. "Thank you for saying that, Gale."

"You and Iris do have something big in common, though." He dipped his chin. "You're both free spirits. I admire that."

Cedar tilted her head just slightly to the side. "Tell me more."

"I never changed my mind about Iris, about choosing her. When we turned eighteen, I was ready to make good on my word. I was ready to make her mine. We had basically been together for a few years before then anyway, figuring out what it means to become an adult and experimenting with sex. I had the future all mapped out. But she left me. She left all of us. She said she didn't want to stay with the clan because she wanted to see the world. She didn't want to stay and live the life everyone expected."

Cedar smiled as she leaned back against a tree. "She certainly sounds like someone I know."

"Iris never talked to me about wanting to leave. I thought we were happy together, and I took her leaving hard. I got depressed and sulked around everywhere. Back then, my parents were the ones in charge of the Loike Clan. They got fed up with me eventually and kicked me out. They told me to find myself and that I wasn't welcome back until I did. So I did. I left Alaska for the main body of the United States. I tried to find that wanderlust Iris had. I knew next to nothing about humans and technology, but I was a quick study. It was the only way to survive outside of the clan, and I became a truck driver. I drove across the country."

"The technology thing was a big slap in the face, don't you think?" Cedar asked. A smile tugged at her lips.

"Yes." Gale laughed. "It wasn't easy at first. I remember a lot of running, hiding, and hoping the humans wouldn't recognize me for something stupid I had done because I didn't know any better."

"Been there." Cedar wore a full-on grin now, complete with a cute dimple on her left cheek. Gale wanted to reach out and touch it, but he trapped his hands behind his back and against the tree trunk. He hadn't grabbed gloves before they stepped outside, but his hands weren't cold even though they were pressed against a sheet of ice. Cedar made him hot. He wasn't buzzing with Solsis this time. It was all her.

Gale cleared his throat. "That was a strange time in my life. It was my first experience being on my own. In some ways, it was nice. In other ways, it was lonely."

The smile vanished from Cedar's face, and Gale guessed she related to that very well herself.

"One day my truck driving led me back to Iris," Gale continued. "Who would've thought? I had stopped for gas, and Iris was there at the gas station with Ling.

That was when I first met Ling. She and Iris were partners, a peacekeeper duo. I'll admit we didn't initially hit it off. I felt threatened by Ling because she and Iris were closer than work partners or friends. I never did learn how far they went, but I know Ling loved Iris the same way I did. In the end, Iris chose me, though—much to my relief. She told me later that it was seeing me again that made her realize she couldn't be with Ling. There was still something between us, and we both felt it, even after we hadn't seen each other in years.

"Iris agreed to come home with me, but it wasn't just about coming home for her. It was about Trinity. She told me all about Trinity, how it could help Eurio and vice versa. She talked about Trinity like the Celestial Alphas are gods meant to save this world. The Toran Pack and Loike Clan were always close neighbors, but we never lived side by side like we do now. It was Iris who laid the foundation for what Eurio is today.

"During our preparations to travel back to Alaska, Iris inadvertently stumbled upon the Lenkov twins. They were fourteen at the time and had been stealing to survive. They were almost caught by the police because of one of Yuri's seizures, but Iris stepped in. They were in a bad way and needed somewhere to stay, so they ended up coming back with us.

"Back home, Iris became mine. I finally tamed a wildfire."

Cedar nodded. "I saw the scar."

Gale's hand went to his left bicep, where Iris had bitten him years ago and marked him as her own. He had done the same to her. She was the territorial type and would have bitten him again if his mark faded too much. She wasn't here to do that anymore, though. The scar would continue to fade, but the memory of her wouldn't.

"I got her pregnant," Gale said. "We were both ecstatic, young mates who still didn't know much about anything despite traveling and seeing more of the world than either of us probably thought possible. But we lost that cub. Iris miscarried. She wouldn't talk to me about it. She set it aside and acted like it never happened, but I know her. It hurt her so much she left again without notice. She left me alone in Eurio to deal with the mess she left us, and a bunch of helpless shifters Trinity had brought to us because they didn't have room.

"I lost myself in that work and slowly found myself in a leadership position. My parents happily stepped down from the Trinity stuff. They were getting on in years, and I knew more about Trinity, how to handle this expansion, how to deal with the technology in Fairbanks, and everything else going on at that point. I never wanted any of it, but it was my own fault for following Iris. It was kind of inevitable it turned out that way when I look back on it. I think it was what Iris had intended from the very beginning.

"In a couple years, my parents taught me everything they knew about leading a clan. And they stepped down, leaving Eurio to me and Weston. Together, we were able to transform Eurio into something bigger. It felt like good work. We all liked the idea of helping shifters who needed us. The Lenkovs were welcomed with open arms before Iris even warmed the rest of Eurio up to the idea of allying with Trinity. We all trusted Iris, and she trusted Trinity. Apparently, that was enough. The peacekeepers we met, the representatives, they were all genuine as far as we could sense."

"A perk of being a shifter," Cedar said. "We're often better than lie detectors."

Gale nodded. "A couple years passed, and Iris finally decided to come back home. She hardly spoke a word to me while she was gone, no phone calls or letters. I had wondered if she had left me or died in a ditch somewhere. The only news I had of her was from Trinity Shifters. Ling became a close friend. I trusted her to look out for my mate, to give me hopeful bits of news that kept me from going insane. So, I waited. I waited and waited patiently for Iris to come back. When she did, I was relieved, but I was angry too."

Gale clenched his fists and gritted his teeth. "I let her know. I blew up. I half-intended to ignore her, to put her through exactly what she had put me through. It would have been petty, but if I were her, it would have worked because I would have broken down and confronted me. But Iris was never like me, and I could never stay mad at her for long.

"I got her pregnant again. She never said it or admitted it, but I think that scared her. She was getting ready to run again. I saw her packing one night, preparing to leave without saying a word to me. I told her to stay. I couldn't go through it again, not when she never even took the time to contact me herself. I knew I couldn't make her do anything, so I resorted to begging. I was always pleading with her. And I talked. I told her we needed to work through the pain of losing our first cub together. We should have done it years ago. We couldn't just bury it and forget about it. I told her I was scared too. Like I said, she never admitted her fear, but she did listen to me. She even stayed. We had Ike. Those were the best months of my life. I had my mate and I got to hold Ike for the first time."

Gale sighed. "But Iris did end up leaving again. This time it wasn't because she was running, and it wasn't without a word. Trinity called her in. It was over some big new find concerning Black Witches. Apparently, they cost Trinity a lot, years before, so they wanted to go in guns blazing. Iris left, and she never came back."

Gale looked up at the snowy tree branches and through to the dark sky. It wasn't so dark now. There were lights beyond the moon and stars, blues, greens, and yellows. They were a dancing ribbon in the sky, illuminating the landscape below with its elusive magic. One never quite knew when an aurora would show face.

Was Iris watching him?

A tear rolled down Gale's cheek. He wiped it away before it could freeze on his skin. "What's it been? Six years since then? Almost seven. A long time. It's been a long time since I lost my mate. I miss her. I wasn't there for Ike at all after I got news of her death. I stopped functioning. My parents had to step up with Ike and Eurio. But everyone kept telling me they needed me.

So, I tried to climb back out of that hole I was stuck in. Believe it or not, Cedar, I've come a long way since then, but I know I'm still basically a useless father. I want to change. Spirits, I'm trying. I just don't know how to bond with Ike. I don't know how to act. I don't know how to move on." He rubbed his eyes. He was exhausted. His chest ached and threatened to fracture, but he refused to shed any more tears.

"I am sorry for what happened. I shouted Iris's name, but it had nothing to do with you. I didn't have sex with you because I was missing my mate and wanted to use you to imagine being with her again." Just the thought of that made him sick to his stomach. "I wanted to be with you, only you. But I started feeling... guilty, I guess. Confused. It was like I was cheating, but I know that's stupid. Iris is gone. I should let her go, but I don't know how to." He looked up at the sky. Iris was gone, but maybe not too far away if spirits really did travel in those bands of light. "You deserve the world, Cedar. Don't ever let anyone tell you otherwise. Don't let some asshole tell you to lose weight or to be something you're not. You're beautiful."

Cedar raised her chin. "I know."

"Anyway, I saw what you did at Weston's today. You work fast, lady. I'm very impressed. You'll have

Eurio organized and running the way Trinity wants in no time. You're like a storm where the opposite happens: instead of destruction and mayhem, you bring organization and unity."

"Hell yeah," she said. "I am the best."

Gale chuckled. "Clearly. Cedar, if there's ever anything you need, don't hesitate to ask."

She looked up at the aurora rippling through the sky. It caught in her eyes, mingling with their naturally dark brown color; it was a rainbow. "Lights," she said. The colors stayed in her eyes as she brought her gaze to Gale.

"Lights?" he asked, barely able to breathe.

"You're taking your son to see the Christmas lights in Fairbanks, and you're going to tell him right now."

"Okay."

"And I'm coming too since you obviously need some guidance."

Gale couldn't stop the smile fighting for control of his lips. "Yes, ma'am."

Perhaps Cedar forgave him after all.

CHAPTER 13

IKE HADN'T BELIEVED HIM. Gale went to his room right after his talk with Cedar and told him they were going to see the Christmas lights in Fairbanks. All Ike could do was stare. He was quiet about it the following days, too; he hadn't brought it up once. But Gale was serious. They were going, and he made sure to bring it up daily, so Ike knew he was serious, for the week it took before they headed out. Ike held on to his reservations until they were physically in the SUV and on their way to Fairbanks. He couldn't contain himself after that, though. He bounced impatiently in his seat and stared out the window, eager to see his father's words become truth.

Cedar had planned it all out, when they were going, what they'd be doing. It wasn't enough for her to just see the lights. She wanted to do some shopping while they were there. Her plan was to bring lights back to Eurio and make decorating the Lodge an activity all residents could participate in. She said it was another opportunity to bring them all together. She also said Ike would probably like it. Gale agreed he probably would and let her do her thing. There was no use telling her no anyway. Cedar also had a grocery list for Christmas dinner, which easily made this an all-day event.

Ike was shy at first with all the people around. He had been around humans before, but it wasn't something he was used to. Cedar knew how to get him to settle, though. It was like her words were magic. Ike's whole face would light up whenever she spoke to him. He had taken quite a liking to the she-bear. Shopping came first on the agenda. Cedar pointed out Christmas decorations available for sale, engaging Ike with each one until he didn't have to be prompted or asked to give his opinion anymore. She made him comfortable.

Gale was almost jealous.

Ike stood in front of one of those reindeer meshes fitted with white lights. "I want you in front of the Lodge," he said. Then he pointed at a dragon, an odd

Christmas decoration, but Christmas nonetheless since it was green and wore a red Santa hat. "And this," Ike said. "The dragon will hunt the reindeer."

Some humans walked by just then, a mother and a father with their child. The mother looked at Ike with wide eyes, and the father laughed. Their child said, "I want a Christmas dragon to hunt our reindeer, too!"

"No!" the mother exclaimed.

Cedar hid a giggle behind her hand. "Gale, you're the one with the budget."

"Sounds good, Ike. Let's get them," Gale replied.

The eager cub grabbed the boxes next to the displays and put them in one of their carts. Cedar was pushing one and Gale was pushing the other.

"I want to push it!" Ike said as he squeezed in between Gale and his cart.

"Can you even see over those boxes?" Boxes were piled high in the carts. It was a bit precarious.

Ike stood on his tiptoes and craned his neck. "Nope."

"You push, I'll steer?"

Ike nodded and pushed. Gale had to quickly grab hold of the cart before his rambunctious cub took out one of the displays.

"Maybe say stop and go so I know what you're doing," Gale said as they narrowly avoided another close call. Cedar was behind them, hand covering her mouth. Her shoulders were shaking, eyes shining. At least someone was getting a good laugh out of this.

"Go!" Ike yelled.

Cedar burst out in laughter this time, and Gale did his best to safely guide Ike to one of the checkout lanes.

Once they were out of the store, a few hours had passed since they had arrived in Fairbanks. The lights were starting to turn on now that it was sufficiently dark. Gale wondered if Ike was conducting some of that electricity coursing through the city because he was bouncing more than usual. Ike was distracted by the lights the whole way to the SUV. He kept looking at them while they put their haul in the trunk.

"Are we leaving already?" he asked.

"Did we see the lights yet?" Gale replied

"No. Yes? I don't know. We saw them on the way to the SUV."

"Doesn't count. We're going to get a proper look at them."

Ike gave a tentative smile, and Gale smiled back. It wasn't hard, and it wasn't forced. For the first time in a long time, Gale's smile was completely genuine. His boy must've seen the difference as much as Gale felt it because Ike grabbed his hand and swung their arms back and forth as he hummed along to "Jingle Bells" playing on a speaker system outside of a shop.

"Let's go!" Ike said.

"We can get hot chocolate while we look around, too," Cedar said. "My treat."

After finding a cute little café and getting that hot chocolate, they took off down the streets. Ike led the way to where the lights were the densest. He took them all the way to a huge Christmas tree in a park. It had a bunch of presents underneath it. They were just decorations of course, but Ike was intrigued.

"Can we have a tree in our own house this year?" he asked. Ike knew enough about Christmas, just like he knew enough about humans, even though he had never celebrated it much himself. It wasn't really a thing in Eurio, but he had been exposed to it when he and Gale lived with Mateo in Utah for a while.

"Sure, we can. When we get back to Eurio, you find the perfect tree, and I'll help you chop it down," Gale said. Ike squeezed his hand a little tighter. He hadn't let go.

"Will Cedar stay forever?" Ike wondered.

"You want me to stay forever?" she asked, disheveling his winter hat as she rubbed his head playfully.

"You make Dad different. And I like you."

Cedar frowned. "I don't know how long I'll be in Eurio, Ike, but I'll always be your friend."

Ike grabbed her hand with his free one. He made sure he had both adults attached to him and pulled them closer. His grip was strong with no intention of letting go. "Please stay."

"You have turned Eurio around, in what, less than a week?" Gale said, coming to his son's aid. "We've all come to rely on you."

"Now you're just being ridiculous," Cedar chided.

But he wasn't. He meant it. In the short time Cedar had been there, she had turned his life around. She lived with him and Ike and brought an order and stability he craved and never had with Iris. He knew she was here for Trinity, and she was doing an excellent job organizing and changing things like Trinity wanted, but it was more than that. Gale was happy to take a backseat. He liked knowing she'd be there when he woke up in the morning, and it was obvious Ike felt the same way.

She made sure they all ate dinner together, and they took turns preparing the food. It was a brand-new and already ingrained routine. They spent quality time together every day, and it was easy. Natural.

Because of her support, for the first time in years, Gale was making waves instead of splashes.

He took his son to school for the first time in weeks yesterday morning. He never liked Ike going to school or coming home by himself, but it was often hard for Gale to get out of bed. This last week, he had more energy than usual. He could talk to Ike and initiate their interactions without shutting down if Ike's reply was cold. The ice was thawing.

Gale loved Iris, but she never gave him the stability Cedar had managed to give him in a week's time. She was too unpredictable. She didn't talk about the important stuff. She left him in pieces more than once. He wasn't like her. They didn't complement each other, and they never had.

It didn't mean he loved Iris any less, but the realization was heavy, an invisible weight on his shoulders.

"You're both flatterers," Cedar said. She swung Ike's hand, bent down, and gave him a kiss on the cheek. "We don't need to worry about this now, okay? We're going to enjoy Christmas. Together. Any specific presents you guys want?"

"You to stay," Ike said.

Apparently, Gale's son was craving stability as

much as he was. It wasn't just that, though. Cedar was a ray of sunshine. She chased the gray clouds away so the flowers could bloom. She was family.

"Ike…" Cedar shook her head. "I'm not going anywhere, okay? You don't need to worry."

"Good," he said, nodding his head. "What do you want for Christmas, Cedar?"

"Anything that comes from this sweet heart of yours." She poked his chest.

He blushed. "Okay."

"Aren't you going to ask me what I want, Gale?"

Gale shrugged, but he was smiling. "What do you want for Christmas, Cedar?"

"Dinner. I want to see everything I've taught you put to good use. Actually, that goes for you too, Ike."

"I've learned a lot. I can do it," the cub said proudly.

"That's what I want to hear."

Gale chuckled. "Deal."

They walked farther into the park, and Ike cut loose. He ran through the snow, unconcerned about whether there was a paved and shoveled trail or not, and up to each display. He touched everything he could as if he saw as much with his hands as his eyes. Gale hadn't seen him smile so much in years. His own cheeks hurt from smiling in response. It was an empathetic reflex he hadn't felt in some time. He was happy that Ike was happy.

Nothing could stop the whirlwind cub until they came to a temporary shelter where an old man dressed as Santa sat inside. Kids were gathered around him, and he was giving away free candy canes. Ike stood just outside of the throng, gray eyes wide.

"Want to go in?" Gale asked. "Free candy canes."

"Too bad we finished our hot chocolate. You could save the candy cane, and I'll make more hot chocolate at home," Cedar suggested. "The peppermint and chocolate taste good together."

"I'm going in," Ike said and puffed out his chest.

Gale gave his back a little push. "You can talk to the other kids, you know?"

Ike nodded, staring straight ahead, eyes on the prize. He had never seen Santa before. That wasn't something he got to do during their time in Utah. Gale wondered if Ike would end up leaving Eurio one day. Did he have the same wanderlust his mother had? He supposed time would tell.

Cedar's gloved hand brushed against Gale's, and he reflexively took it. He was prepared for her to pull away or to protest, but she didn't. She let him hold her hand. She even laced her fingers with his. He worked up the courage to look at her. She had a soft smile on her face as she watched Ike. She wasn't looking at him, but Gale was sure she could see him out of her peripheral vision.

"I've decided," she said.

"Decided what?" Gale held his breath.

"I'm going to teach you how to control Solsis. You accessed it once, so it's going to show itself again eventually, and it's not enough for me to babysit you and make sure you don't burn the town down when it does. Besides, it'll be good for you as an Alpha of Eurio. You'll have more power, so you'll be a better protector if times call for it. Maybe It'll help you understand Trinity better, too."

"Is this exclusive or will Ike be babysitting?" Gale wasn't sure why he asked that. Probably because he hoped this meant he'd get to spend more time alone with Cedar. The heat rushing to his core with the look she gave him next only confirmed that notion. He wanted this she-bear. And her sweet scent meant she still wanted him, too. At least, her body did. Now he had to win her heart. That was the hard part, but he wanted to try. She had already won his. Ike's too.

"Exclusive," she said, bumping him with a full hip.

"I look forward to it," Gale said. He took her hand laced in his and gently peeled off her glove. She raised an eyebrow but allowed him to continue. Once her skin was exposed to the cold, he kissed the back of her hand. Heat deepened the color in her cheeks. Her sweet scent flooded into his nostrils.

"Me too," she whispered. "Me too."

CHAPTER 14

"**THE LODGE LOOKS COMPLETELY** different now!" Ike said.

"Is that a good thing?" Cedar asked.

"Yeah! It's like Fairbanks. There are so many lights. This is going be the best Christmas in Eurio ever."

"The first one really," Gale mused.

Cedar was enjoying this new routine. Walking with both Gale and Ike on their way to school in the morning was a family-like activity she hadn't been a part of for some years. But she was working on that. Seeing Gale and Ike made her realize she didn't want to leave her relationships the way they were. She wrote a letter to her parents and her siblings. It would take a while to get to them. It wouldn't have even been possible to send them a letter if not for Trinity. She was lucky for that, and she hoped this would be the start of them talking again. She had left on less than good terms and wasn't part of the clan anymore, but nothing would happen if she didn't try. She hoped they could put aside their differences after all this time apart.

"Bye, Dad. Bye, Cedar. See you after school!" Ike called as he ran for the door. Before disappearing inside, he turned around and waved sporadically. He was smiling without reservation. Cedar had seen this kid transform in the short time she had been in Eurio. A couple weeks now. Things had settled down since that first day. Way too much happened in that first day. This kind of steady progress was a lot better for her health.

"Another day of training?" Gale asked.

"Another day of training," Cedar agreed. "To the Tanana River."

She walked side by side with Gale through endless snow, and their hands brushed against each other. But he didn't make a move. Gale hadn't taken her hand again since that day in Fairbanks. She didn't want to admit that it disappointed her. She didn't want to admit that she wanted to hold his hand. Well, part of her did.

That day she had sex with him was one of the craziest moments of her life, but he had been nothing but a pure gentleman since. He also gave her a sincere apology almost right away. She was still attracted to him and was certain that wouldn't change, but it had been transforming into much more than a physical thing for her since spending so much time with him. Much more. She liked living with him and Ike. She liked being a part of this family. She liked how it had changed since she arrived, how it kind of felt like they'd always been here together.

They complemented each other.

"How are you feeling about Solsis today?" Cedar asked.

"Solid, but you haven't given me a day off. You've worked me to the bone to make sure of that. You can be a real pain in the ass, Cedar. It's like I'm in fucking boot camp. Are you sure you're not actually a peacekeeper?" Gale deadpanned.

She laughed. "No peacekeeper here. Have you seen my rather disappointing display of muscle?" She held out her arm and flexed. It wasn't impressive. It also didn't help that her coat was puffy and well insulated. If Gale hadn't seen her naked body before, he would've had just a foggy idea of what she looked like underneath.

He played along, though. He placed his big hand on her bicep and squeezed playfully. "Way too much muscle for me."

Cedar smirked. "You ain't seen nothing yet."

"Have mercy."

She lightly swatted at him, and he held up his arms in self-defense.

At the icy riverbank, Gale proceeded to strip off his clothes. He left on his boots and pants, but the coat, scarf, hat, gloves, and everything else was discarded on the ground.

"Show me what you've got," Cedar said as she stripped down to nothing but her boots, pants, and a tank top.

Gale started with his hand. He held it out, fingers extended. He focused only on that area like Cedar had taught him. His brown skin began to glow, golden-hued at first, brighter and brighter, until it was a bright white and painful to look at. Then he dimmed it. The white went away, and the glowing stopped, leaving only his natural skin tone behind.

"Excellent," Cedar praised. "Think you can handle your entire torso?"

Gale didn't comment. He got right to it instead. He curled his hands into fists and pressed them together in front of his chest, elbows spread out wide. His entire torso lit up like his hand had. It was a heatless flame since Cedar had taught him how to keep Solsis from leaking. Soon it was blinding. He brought the Sun Magic to the point of near-explosion, and then he brought it back down with astonishing precision. To be honest, he was getting better at this than Cedar was. She kind of hated that, but it also made sense. Yeah, she was an excellent fisher, but that was the extent of her "combat" skills. Fighting wasn't her forte. Gale didn't exactly seem like a fighter either, but he was probably closer to one than she was. She wasn't hard to beat there.

"I don't think there's anything left for me to teach you," Cedar grumbled. "You learn too fast. I have no idea why I bothered bringing you out here today."

"I guess you just wanted to make sure I had this," Gale said. "Besides, I'm not complaining. I like spending time with you."

Those words transformed into the sudden heat in Cedar's cheeks. "You do?" There was heat in between her thighs, too. It focused there along with an almost painful throbbing.

"Very much." He glanced at her. He didn't look for long, but Cedar knew he was aware of her nearly constant arousal. He hadn't commented on it, though. He hadn't brought up sex once since he apologized.

"Gale, can we talk?"

He focused on the snow underfoot. "Sure."

"Don't act all nervous. It's nothing bad."

Gale let out a breath, making a big show of it. He grinned at her afterward. He and Ike had the same smile.

"You told me about you and Iris. You trusted me with something important: your feelings. I think it's only fair I did the same. I mean, I've had you at a bit of a disadvantage anyway with all of that Trinity intelligence I came here with."

"You have indeed."

Cedar stood by the edge of the frozen river and stared at the cracks and clear sections between opaque white. "I grew up in a polar bear clan even more secluded than yours. We didn't have any neighbors like the Toran Pack. I had parents and siblings who loved me, and life was great when I was young. The seclusion didn't matter. But when I got older, mating age, I decided that the things I wanted didn't align with what was expected of me. I wasn't interested in finding a mate—mostly because I hated that females were expected to stay with their cubs while the males of our clan went out hunting and fishing when I was the best fisher there. It didn't make sense. So it put me off to mates entirely. It wasn't about monogamy or anything like that."

"I can see why. You're not lying about your fishing skills," Gale said. "I'll never delude myself into thinking I can beat you at that again."

Cedar laughed. Then she wrapped her arms around her middle as a cold breeze floated by, and she kicked against the icy ground. She thought about grabbing her coat, but the chill felt good for some reason. It made her outsides match her insides.

She said, "I left one day. I decided to see what was out there because I didn't know. I had heard about humans and their technology from my clan bad-talking them, but I wasn't quite prepared for it when I was confronted with it all. I got through it, though, and I learned a lot. Luckily for me, a Trinity shifter named Isabelle found me soon after. She helped me find a place in the human world and taught me about Trinity, too. I was fascinated by it right away. I couldn't believe there was this big group of shifters with their roots spread far and wide, working side by side with humans, without humans even knowing it. I ended up joining them, and that led me to where I am today. I'm convinced nothing better could have happened to me when I left home.

"I had always been kind of self-conscious about my looks, too. I'm just bigger. Bigger even than most bear shifters. You know? Guess that didn't stop me from experimenting or anything. I'm a sucker for a guy with a hot body, but it never went anything beyond sex. Sometimes it was fine, satisfying, but it's the bad times that stick out in my mind. Guys telling me to lose weight, that I'd look prettier, that I have potential. They were always human males for me, a step removed from mates, I guess. I don't want to change for anyone else, but sometimes it still hurts." She pressed her fingers together. "That's stupid, huh?"

"No. It's not stupid. But those guys are idiots. You're beautiful just the way you are, Cedar," Gale said. Then he smirked. "I do think all the hiking you've been doing in Eurio has done you some good, though. Your endurance was terrible when you first got here—and you *still* beat me at fishing."

Cedar put her hands on her hips. "I'm just that good." She wasn't going to disagree with what he said, though. She was super out of shape compared to what she had been in her clan. She had been doing desk jobs since joining Trinity and lost the active lifestyle she had had before. She hadn't missed it until recently. She could feel the difference—though she wasn't a fan of being sore. But it would fade. She could endure. How else would she keep up with Ike? How else would she keep up with Gale if they got together again? Hell, she wanted to go hard. And, damn it, she was wet.

She walked back from the very edge of the river, closing the small distance between her and Gale. "You really like me the way I am?"

"Definitely," he said. His voice was low. She wouldn't have heard him if she hadn't stood on her tip-toes to get close.

She reached up and around his neck, resting her hands on the back of it. She tugged, inviting him to reach down, acting as if she might kiss him. Maybe she would. Gale's eyes moved back and forth between hers before settling. He leaned down cautiously. But then Cedar pulled back. She took both of his hands, yanked him forward with the new strength she had acquired here, and thrust his hands into the water.

"Use what I taught you," she said.

Gale lit up his hands.

Cedar moved back. "Let it go."

Gale allowed the Sun Magic to reach white-hot. Ice melted, water began to sizzle, and steam rose into the air in big hissing puffs as it burst. Water shot up like a geyser mingling with the steam. Cedar couldn't see more than an inch in front of her face until it settled and everything froze into stillness once again.

When Gale brought his hands back out of the water to shake them off, she took advantage of him being hunched over. She grabbed his hands, pulled him into her, and kissed him. His body was tense with surprise, but it quickly melted away. Cedar's tight grip also melted away. She allowed him to move. He kept one hand in hers and used the other to adjust the way her head was angled with a soft touch on her chin. He kissed her deeper, and he took his time. There was a latent hunger that grew with each passing second, but it was different from the time he had kissed her with the intention of having sex with no strings attached. This kiss was a question for more.

He caressed her lips with his own, over and over, like he couldn't get enough of her. Cedar nipped at his bottom lip. Her tongue darted inside of his mouth, tasting him again after what felt like ages.

"I think I can forgive you," she whispered.

Gale moved back. His eyebrows shot up in surprise.

"What?" Cedar asked. "Did I say something wrong?" She could smell his arousal, too. She thought they were on the same page.

"No." He breathed. "You didn't say or do anything wrong. I just don't want to fuck up again. I still have things to work through, Cedar. With Iris and letting her go." He touched her cheek. "Will you give me more time?"

"Well, I guess I'm not planning on going anywhere," she said quietly.

Gale bit his lip. "I'd be lying if I said I didn't want to keep you, Cedar." His eyes were glossy.

"Keep me?" she whispered.

"Yes, keep you."

"I said I didn't want to be a breeder."

"Cedar, I'd never ask you to be a breeder. I'd never tell you you weren't allowed to do something. Keeping you... I mean it like this." He took her hand and pressed her palm flat against his chest. "I want to keep you here."

Her cheeks burned hotter. "I don't hate kids or anything. I adore Ike. I mean, just so you know that wasn't what I meant. Oh, god. I'm going to shut up now."

Gale chuckled. "I know. Ike adores you, too."

Cedar hugged him partly to hide the embarrassment showing on her face and partly because she wanted to feel him. He wrapped his arms around her, stroked her long black hair, and kissed her forehead. His touch was addicting. "Why do you feel so good?" she asked.

"That's my line."

She smiled into his bare chest. It was cold as cold outside, but she couldn't feel anything outside of his arms. She wanted this always. She wanted to "keep" him, too.

"I'm not going anywhere," she said. "You'll figure this out, Gale. You'll find a way to be happy again. I know you will. Until then, don't forget those who care about you. I care about you. You can lean on us when you're not strong enough to stand on your own."

He held her tighter. "I am happy. Happier than I've been in a long time."

"Happier than that."

He nipped at her ear. "You have no idea how much I want you."

"Want me?" she teased. She pushed back and looked up at him. His eyes were on her lips. "How do you want me?"

"In," he kissed her, "every," he sucked on her lower lip, "way." He locked his gaze onto hers. "If you leave, this place won't be the same. If you leave, I won't be the same. You're family, Cedar. You've changed me, brought me closer to my son, settled this restless energy inside of me, and taught me how to use Solsis. Whatever you decide you want to do after your assignment here is done, I will never forget you. You've got a permanent place in my heart. You have a home here if you want it."

Cedar pressed her hand to his chest again, right over his heart. She closed her eyes and focused on the steady rhythm of his heartbeat. She had fallen in love.

"Sorry to interrupt."

Cedar cleared her throat and backed away from Gale, suddenly self-conscious, as she looked out at the trees beyond the riverbank to where Weston stood, leaning against a tree trunk.

"We have a visitor," he said.

Standing beside him was the White Witch Cedar had called in: Josh. Weston was giving Cedar a hard look. His eyes were pitch-black. It might have made her shiver if she hadn't held strong in her convictions. She did the right thing.

Gale's body went rigid. The soft connection was

gone, and his fingers were hard on her arms, digging into her skin. He growled, and the sour scent of unease permeated his skin. "What's this about? Who are you?"

He must have sensed the spark of magic coming from Josh. It was hard to pinpoint, and a shifter wouldn't know what it was without experiencing it, but it had a way of offsetting the nerves. It was instinct, a reaction to the unknown.

"Gale, this is Josh. I asked him to come here for Yuri." Cedar lightly touched Gale's arm. He was shaking. His lips set into a firm and grim line.

"You invited a *witch* here?"

"Josh is one of the best *healers* I know."

Gale tried to look away from her, but she caught his face in her hands. He still could've decided not to look at her, but he reluctantly met her eyes, allowing her hands to guide him.

"It's not a good idea," he said. "I don't like witches, but the Lenkovs *hate* them. I tried to bring one in before, when you first arrived and I took you to their cabin."

So that was what they were signing about, Cedar thought.

"Yuri keeps getting worse, and everyone knows it.

But the tiger twins don't want to try anything that includes a witch. I understand their feelings, even if I don't know what the hell they experienced in the past to make them feel that way. They won't talk about it."

"How often have you seen Yuri in the last week?" Cedar asked.

Gale said nothing.

"Not at all, right? Lance says everything is fine, but he's lying. Everyone lets him lie because there's no way he'd ever do anything that would hurt his brother, because you don't like witches. You all need to get over yourselves and ask for help. Yuri is bad sick, and it's not going to get better. There's only one thing you haven't tried, and that's asking a White *Witch* for help."

Gale flinched. "You're dangerous, Cedar."

"I do what I have to."

Gale held up his hands reticently.

"Cedar, what kind of mess did you bring me into?" Josh called from the tree line. He ran a hand over his bald head and down his face.

"Nothing you're not used to." She smiled sweetly.

Josh shook his head. "So, where's the shifter in need of my help?"

CHAPTER 15

GALE WASN'T HAPPY.

He trusted Cedar and felt like she had good intentions. He meant what he said about keeping her and about her being family. But why had she kept this from him? How long ago had she called this witch in? It wasn't like Trinity had witches on call. This took some time to arrange.

He couldn't believe it. Cedar had always been so upfront about everything. She ran it by him and Weston whenever she wanted to change how anything in Eurio was run. She let them know exactly what she was doing with their records and what she was sending off to Trinity and why. They gave her permission to work on their records and organize things as she saw fit after a while. That was all well and good, but bringing in a White Witch was a breach in their power structure. She wasn't an Alpha here. Gale didn't blame Weston for bowing out of this one. Besides, the Lenkovs didn't like being cornered. Lance in particular.

Gale knocked on the Lenkovs' door. He wasn't going to burst in today.

He didn't like witches. He didn't like them at all. They were the reason Iris was dead. He knew there was a difference between Black Witches and White Witches. He knew that Trinity worked with White Witches and that they utilized a very different kind of magic, but it was hard for him to be around Josh. His smell made Gale's nose tickle. It was the kind of tickle that wouldn't go away, like he had to sneeze but couldn't. He could hardly look at the man with the shiny bald head.

"Lance, open up," Cedar demanded as she knocked impatiently, unsatisfied with Gale's weak attempt.

The door swung open. "What do you wa—" Lance quickly scanned them over, and his eyes rested on Josh. Gale held out his hand to catch the door and keep it open, but he wasn't quick enough. Lance slammed it in their faces. Typical.

"Go the hell away before I lose my shit," the dismembered and muffled voice of the tiger shifter on the other side of the door warned.

"You're already mad," Gale replied. "Might as well open up and face us. Josh is a *White* Witch, Lance. If anyone can help Yuri, he can. White Magic is the only thing we haven't tried. I told you about this befo—"

"Shut up, Gale. We're not doing magic. No one should be able to do that shit!"

"I started using Solsis. You know about that, right? Does that mean you don't want me around anymore?" Gale asked.

Lance didn't say anything.

"Please, Lance. Don't be mad at Gale," Cedar said. "Bringing Josh here was my idea. I didn't ask anybody for permission. I made this decision on my own. After we went sledding and I saw Yuri's seizure, I had to make a choice. We only want to help."

"You can inspect me thoroughly if it'll put you at ease," Josh added.

"Fuck no!" Lance said. "No witches. Go away."

Gale said, "You've known me for years. Don't you trust me?"

"I know that you're as fucked up as we are."

"A better reason to trust me then. I know where you're coming from. Did you have an encounter with a witch, Lance? You know my mate was killed by Black Witches. Iris. She saved you." Gale grimaced. "You and Yuri didn't like to talk about how you ended up on your own. You told us you'd been on your own for years and that Yuri had been dealing with the seizures all his life. Is that true or are you leaving out important details?"

"What else is there to tell?" Lance growled. "Yuri's sick and the seizures are slowly killing him. You've seen it for yourself."

Yes, Gale had. He was there through the difficult adjustment of Yuri no longer able to hold a conversation because he just couldn't understand the words. It changed him. Understandably. It wasn't getting through another seizure. It was almost like losing one of his senses. Things had stabilized after that. Until recently.

"Let Josh see Yuri. White Magic could cure him. We tried everything else. We did everything else first. This is all we have left. I know you've been researching day and night, but what can you do that a doctor hasn't? It's time to get off your high horse. Talk to your brother if you have to. Convince him to let Josh take a look at him."

"You don't understand."

"Help us to," Cedar urged.

The three of them waited outside of the Lenkovs' cabin. An icy wind blew by, but beyond that, it was silent as death. Minutes passed, but they stayed. Gale could sense Lance's presence on the other side of the door. He hadn't moved. Gale hoped that meant something.

"A monster did this to Yuri," Lance said the words so quietly they almost couldn't be heard; Josh probably hadn't caught them since he didn't have heightened senses like a shifter. "A monster killed our dad and did this to Yuri." He said that last part louder.

"What do you mean by that? A 'monster'?" Josh asked. Gale noticed the witch's eye twitch and his lips curve down just slightly.

Lance and Yuri had never said anything about a monster before, not when Iris found them and saved them. All this time and they hadn't been telling the truth. It was aggravating, but Gale wasn't surprised. The twins were chronic liars, and they had a closeness with each other that they didn't have with anyone else. They didn't let anyone in. Only Mateo came close.

"Before Iris found us, before everything, the first

thing I can remember is me and Yuri with our dad trying to find work in the states. He brought us here from Russia. Never did learn why, and I was too young to care. I don't know what happened to our mom. Don't even remember her. And Dad never talked about it. The year was two thousand and five, coming out of winter. Our little family always struggled because nobody wanted to employ our dad. He spoke broken English, we were dirty, didn't have a permanent residence. I think we might have been *illegal aliens*."

They weren't US citizens. Gale could attest to that, but Iris had taken care of all of that too when she found them. Trinity did these tigers some big favors despite getting nothing in return. That was when Gale realized just how powerful Trinity was. It was also when Trinity got Gale's respect.

"But we were okay," Lance murmured. "We always found a way no matter what. Dad was resourceful like that. He didn't give up until he was forced to. One day, without warning, we were doing nothing but minding our own business in a back alley of some podunk town in Washington we were living in because nobody had told us to leave yet, and a monster came out of nowhere. It all happened within the span of, like, two seconds. That was my first experience with Black

Magic.

"The monster shot lightning out of his fingertips. It was black at its center, bright even though it was dark. He killed our dad, fried him. And then he turned on Yuri. He was going to kill my brother too, but he didn't. As soon as Yuri screamed, he stopped. I don't know if he was drunk or what, but he slowly slunk away after that, hit the corner of a couple dumpsters on his way out, and I went to my brother. I didn't think he'd wake up. But he did, and I thought he might be okay. Our dad was dead, but we still had each other, and we were survivors. We moved on.

"Then Yuri started with the seizures not long after. They got progressively worse. Every time it happened, I could only see the monster. It has to be the monster's fault my brother is broken."

"Can you describe the monster?" Josh asked.

"He was big and smelled like a wolf, but also something else that stung my nose. He had a moon on his forehead that glowed bright sometimes, and then it would flicker off. Had a shit ton of tattoos, bright eyes… I don't know. I mostly remember the moon." Lance growled. "He kind of smelled like you, *witch*."

Cedar tensed.

"The moon on his forehead is all I needed to

know," Josh said solemnly. "I know who you're talking about, Lance. He *is* a monster. You're lucky you and Yuri survived. But this monster does not reflect all witches. Nor does he reflect all shifters."

"What?" Gale asked. "Who is this guy?"

"A shifter-witch hybrid. A monster created by the Circle. That's all you need to know."

Gale didn't like that answer. He looked to Cedar, hoping she would feel differently. But she averted her gaze. "Cedar."

"It's better if you don't know any more than you have to. Eurio is allied with Trinity, not Trinity itself. Remember?"

"But this guy attacked one of *mine*."

Cedar pursed her lips, but Gale chose the right words. She told him. "Luc Lenoir. That's his name. He almost destroyed Trinity. It happened before I joined."

Josh frowned.

"How?" Gale asked.

"Trinity let him inside. They gave him a chance because of that Moon Mark on his forehead. The current Moon Alpha shares that same mark," Josh said.

"Lunas, right? Moon Magic?"

"Yes, but as I said, Luc is as much a witch as he is a shifter. Darkness won. For whatever reason, he didn't kill Yuri, but it sounds like he cursed him. White Magic is the only thing that can help." Josh pressed his palm flat against the door. "I understand that you're scared, Lance. You're afraid that more magic will make Yuri worse, but I give you my word—no—I'll give you my life. I will do everything I can for your brother. If I can't heal him, you may do with me as you please."

"Josh!" Cedar exclaimed. "You don't know for sure if you can heal him."

"This is important. My life is worth it. I'm one of the best healers Trinity has and the most experienced. If I can't do this on my own, we have a new witch who is far more talented than I. I'll call for help, but I won't give you her life. I can't take her away from her mate."

"*Mate?*" Lance scoffed. "Witches call their lovers mates, too?"

"No, she's mated to a wolf shifter."

"What the actual fuck? Didn't you just finish telling us about your little monster hybrid? Why would Trinity allow something like that?"

"They love each other. It's not about hybrids. It wasn't Trinity's choice."

Lance laughed. Gale wasn't sure he was laughing at first. It started low, under his breath, and then it grew louder, nearly hysterical.

"Is what I offered acceptable, Lance?" Josh asked.

"No. It's not. If you come in here and kill my brother, I'll have nothing left. Killing you in return won't be good enough. It won't matter." The door let out a dull thud from Lance's side, but it stayed closed. "No," the tiger repeated. His voice quavered.

Lance joked about things, had a sharp tongue, and was sarcastic as hell, but it was all a facade. Gale knew that, but it didn't make this breakdown easier to deal with. Something was caught in Gale's throat.

"No one should be able to do things like that," Lance cried. "No one should be able to pick apart my brother's brain like that!"

"You know firsthand the awful things Black Magic can do," Josh said. "Do you know anything about White Magic?"

Lance didn't respond.

Josh continued, "White Magic is healing. Nothing about White Magic is meant for destruction or harming others. By the very nature of White Magic, anything I do would only reinforce your brother's brain and build on the good parts. I want to see if I can chase that Black Magic away, too. You know I'm telling the truth, don't you? Shifters are good at that."

"I think you believe what you're saying, and it

makes me angry."

"Lance, please open up," Gale implored. "I would never let anybody hurt you two. I'll stay with you and Josh the entire time if you want. Josh never has to be alone with Yuri."

"That's right," the witch agreed.

"Yuri's condition was caused by Black Magic. If you had told us the truth sooner, we wouldn't have wasted so much time. Only White Magic is going to fix this. Not doctors, not endless hours of research, nothing. *You* can't fix him." Gale knew his words were harsh, but Lance needed to hear them. He needed to know this was bigger than him.

"Okay?" Gale asked, urging Lance when he had remained quiet. He placed his hand on the door then, ready to knock the damn thing down if Lance didn't cooperate.

"Okay already! Fuck it all." Lance opened the door. Heat leaked out of the cabin, thick like fog. Lance was in nothing but his boxers again. His shoulders shook. His sweaty, tattoo-covered chest puffed in and out as he struggled to breathe.

Gale grabbed Lance's shoulders and pulled him forward, hugging him tightly. "You stubborn tiger. Enough is enough. It's okay to ask for help."

Lance allowed Gale to hold him for just a few seconds before he angrily pushed away and wiped at his watery eyes. "He's asleep. I'll take you to him."

"Thank you, Lance." Josh said.

"You come too, Gale."

"You got it."

"Is it all right if I come, Lance?" Cedar asked.

Lance's eyes flickered over her, but his head bobbed up and down in a yes.

They navigated around all the piles of papers, books, and random scattered computer bits on their way to the twins' room. Yuri was sound asleep on the bed. Those dark circles under his eyes left his skin deeply bruised like he had been in a fight that had given him two black eyes.

"What is all of that stuff outside?" Josh asked, but his eyes were on Yuri, already working to assess his condition. "You've got an entire library in your cabin."

"Research," Lance muttered. "I thought I could save Yuri on my own, but it's been years and nothing. If you can really help him…"

Yuri stirred, taking in a shuddering breath. His skin was slick with sweat, but he shivered underneath his blankets.

"How long has he been like this?" Gale forced his

voice to stay low, but he felt like screaming. "Can you wake him?"

"Better not to. He's been in pain all day." Lance sat down on the floor and wiped the sweat from his brother's brow. "I brought a White Witch to take a look at you, bro. I swore I'd never let another witch touch you again, but I don't know what else to do. You can't leave me like this." He got on his knees and rested his chin on his brother's pillow. "I know it's supposed to be just you and me, but I can't save you. I've tried, but I can't...," a tear fell from his eye, "I can't save you."

"You never told Mateo about this either, did you?" Gale said.

"No. He would've told you. And—"

"You've lived in Eurio for ten years and you've never really trusted any of us, have you?"

Lance shrugged as well as he could without changing his position. Gale could hardly look at him. He knew the dead look on Lance's face all too well. It was the exact reflection he saw of himself when he looked in the mirror after Iris's death. Like he would never be okay again. Like he was dead, too.

Gale couldn't think about that. He couldn't be weak right now. The Lenkovs needed him. They had needed him for a long time, and he hadn't been there.

Maybe if he hadn't been so preoccupied with his own problems, they could have gotten to this point sooner. Now all he could do was hope and pray Josh got here in time to save Yuri.

"You're not alone anymore, Lance. Let us help you," Gale whispered. "After all this goddamn time, let us help you."

And he knew those words applied to him, too. No one could help them unless they let them.

Their biggest enemy had been themselves all along.

CHAPTER 16

"LANCE!"

Cedar stood, meaning to intercept Mateo before he charged in. But he had already barged through the front door and into the Lenkovs' bedroom. It was getting crowded, but it wasn't sweltering anymore. Cedar insisted they crack open a window.

Mateo wasted no time pushing past everyone to get to Lance, who was sitting next to the bed with his hand in Yuri's. Josh sat in a wooden chair. His hands were extended, glowing warm and soft on Yuri's forehead. Wisps of White Magic sunk into Yuri's skin and drifted up in fading particles that resembled snow. Josh's eyes were closed, lost in concentration.

Mateo plopped down on the ground next to Lance. Lance didn't acknowledge his presence; his eyes were locked onto his brother. Cedar hadn't been staring so intensely, but every time she looked at Yuri, she noticed a change in his skin. The bruises under his eyes were lighter, and his face almost had a healthy glow. It was more than that, though. Josh's White Magic wasn't focused on her, but it filled the room with a calming air that affected all of them.

"Why didn't you tell me about this?" Mateo squeezed Lance's arm and growled. "I thought we were 'brothers.'"

"We are!" Lance said. "I'm not good at this shit, okay?" Finally, he ripped his eyes away from his brother long enough to see the grimace on Mateo's face. His own face nearly crumpled in response. He rested his forehead on Mateo's shoulder and didn't say another word. Mateo let him and held the back of his head, pressing his fingers into his short white-blond hair.

"Gale must've called you when he stepped out earlier," Lance murmured.

"I did. I wanted to make sure you had either me or him here with you at all times." Gale said.

"Always playing at being the Alpha."

"I am an Alpha. It's not playing."

Lance grunted.

Josh opened his eyes. The White Magic engulfing his hands disappeared as he leaned back in the chair. He sighed. "That's it for today. I need to recharge, and Yuri could use a break, too. I'll get back to it tomorrow. If I do this for a few hours every day, I should be able to neutralize all of the Black Magic. I'm not sure how many days it will take, though. The Black Magic is rooted deep inside of him, stemming from his brain as I figured. It's had years to grow. But I am confident he will get better."

"That's good news!" Mateo said. "Did you hear that, Lance?" He managed to get a hold of Lance's hair and gently tugged him back to get a look at his face.

"Yeah, I heard that." Lance extracted himself from Mateo's hold. He climbed onto the bed next to his brother and wrapped an arm around him. He pressed his nose against Yuri's cheek. Yuri was on his back, sleeping like he wasn't aware of the world at all. Cedar almost missed the sigh that escaped his lips. He had to be aware of his twin next to him. Lance's touch soothed him like a balm.

Mateo took the chair after Josh stood up to stretch. Mateo put his hand on Lance's shoulder, and his eyes flickered yellow. His hand trembled, but then it was gone.

"A word, Cedar?" Josh said. "Outside."

"All right."

"Wait," Gale said before Cedar could leave the room. "You can go ahead and have your secret conversation, but I'd appreciate it if you told me about anything important you might discuss. You know, anything concerning me or the shifters in my care."

He was angry Cedar hadn't told him about Josh before. She didn't blame him, and she realized she was in the wrong. He would've agreed with her if she had talked to him about it. She hadn't needed to do this behind his back, but she hadn't trusted him enough at the time, and now she had to deal with the consequences.

"I will, Gale, I won't hide anything from you again. That's a promise. Even if I think it's best to keep it to myself, even if I'm trying to do the right thing, I know better now. I know you'll listen. I'm sorry for doubting you before and hurting you because of it." In Cedar's experience, it was better to come clean and speak about issues right away than letting them fester. Unfortunately, it didn't guarantee things would resolve the way she wanted. She had tried talking to her family too, about her feelings on their clan traditions. Maybe they would listen now that she was reaching out to them again with that letter she sent, but it hadn't worked the first time.

Gale folded his arms and leaned back against the wood wall. "I appreciate that."

Cedar touched his arm. "I am sorry."

"I believe you." He took her hand and kissed the back of it. "Go on. I trust you."

Tears stung her eyes, and her chest compressed. She sniffled. "Thank you."

He smiled. It didn't reach his eyes like it had when it was just the two of them at the Tanana River, but it was warm. He didn't hate her.

"I'll be back soon," she promised.

Cedar looked around the house for Josh, but he was nowhere to be seen. None of the stacks of books had collapsed. The intact computer was off and silent. He hadn't been crushed in one of those hoarder avalanches she had heard about on TV, so she looked out the window. Sure enough, Josh was standing outside in the snow with his hands in his coat pockets.

She grabbed her coat, slipped on her gloves and hat, and joined him.

"I was worried for nothing." Josh's eyes were trained on the reddish-gray sky. There were clouds as far as the eye could see. The sun was getting lower and lower, leaving this little part of the world a bit colder. Perhaps it would snow again.

"What do you mean?" Cedar asked. "Is he doing that well?"

Josh shook his head. "I didn't lie in there. He'll get his health back, but I'm not sure I'll be able to restore his brain to what it was before the seizure that caused his PWD. The seizure was caused by the Black Magic tainting his brain, but what happened because of the seizure was because of the seizure itself. Honestly, it's better news than I could have hoped for. When I heard Luc Lenoir was involved in this, I wasn't sure what to expect or what kind of damage I would find once I dove in. I wasn't sure I'd be enough."

"You could have fooled me with how confident you were before."

Josh gave a weak smile. "I've picked up a few things working alongside shifters for many years. I know how to lie in a way that can trick any shifter. You tell lies based on truths. I meant what I said to Lance, but I had to bolster my words and make them sound better than I felt so I could convince him to let me help his brother."

"I'm glad you're on our side." Cedar raised an eyebrow. "You're Trinity's best and most-trusted witch."

"One of them, yes. I know much about White Magic, but Luc Lenoir is much more powerful than I am—and it's not because he uses Black Magic. Witches often grow stronger as they age and as they practice White or Black Magic, but we each have a point we can't surpass. Luc's potential far exceeds mine. However, the Black Magic I found inside of Yuri wasn't anything special. And by that, I mean it wasn't intentional like a curse.

"Strange, isn't it? Yuri was most likely brushed by a high concentration of Black Magic, and so it clung to him and seeded deep inside of his brain. That's bad, but because the Black Magic wasn't focused on him, it would have been easily reversible had a White Witch looked at him right away. Time has allowed that dark seed to grow, so it'll take longer, but I'll still be able to erase every trace of it without much potential needed. In theory, Trinity's youngest and most inexperienced witches would be able to handle this.

"But at this point, with as out of hand as the Black Magic has become, it's for the best I'm the White Witch here for the job. Experience and patience are the keys now. The dark seed has been slowly killing Yuri all these years, using his life force as nutrients to grow. It's amazing he hasn't died. His brain has all but been consumed by it. He's a real fighter. Since he's lasted this long on his own, I'm confident he'll get through this cleansing, too. He just has to hang on a little longer. Each time I treat him, there'll be less Black Magic for him to fight."

"You're determined," Cedar said.

"I hate injustice."

"And you never pass up an opportunity to show reluctant shifters that not all witches are bad."

He smiled at that. "Yes, it's always important to prove that people of any kind aren't automatically a certain way just because of their background, race, species, whatever. We all come from different places, even if we have similarities that tie us together. We categorize things to more easily make sense of them, but it doesn't account for all the variables, all the branches of everything. The world isn't so simple."

Cedar smiled and shook her head. "It's good to see you again, Josh. Thank you for doing this."

Josh cupped his chin with his hand and stared down at the snow. He shoveled away a big chunk of it with his boot, making a large pile on the side. He did it again, moving to different sections to grow his pile. "It is strange, though. Why would Luc kill the Lenkovs' father in such a frenzy and suddenly stop when he got to the boys? If he had just forgotten about them, that might have been one thing. But Lance said he attacked Yuri and then immediately stopped, without warning, when Yuri cried out. It's strange. When he was allowed into Trinity, it was under special circumstances. He and Viktoriya... Well, you know the story."

"The guy's probably insane." Cedar shrugged.

"In any case, it would be wise to report this back to Trinity. It happened years ago, but Viktoriya will want to know." He frowned. "Even though it might be better if she didn't."

Cedar couldn't add to that thought. She wasn't that high up. She had rarely talked to the Celestial Alphas herself. She had seen them before, from time to time, but it was different for Josh. He was the first White Witch to join Trinity. In her opinion, he held rank just below the Celestial Alphas.

"There's something else, Cedar," Josh said. "We might finally be close to getting some answers. We've picked up a clue that might turn into a solid lead. We're following a trail and haven't lost it yet. The Circle is tricky, but patience was bound to yield results eventually. No one is perfect."

"You mean an *actual* trail?" Cedar asked. "Trinity is tracking someone?"

"Yes. One of the Black Witches responsible for massacring Iris's team."

A shiver ran down Cedar's spine. Iris? Gale would want to hear about this. This must've been why Josh wanted to talk to her alone.

"Trinity needs this. It's been too long since we've had anything solid, and the Circle hasn't stopped whatever it is they're trying to do. They're always one step ahead of us."

"How did you find this trail? Has anyone with Terros Sight *seen* this witch? The Earth Alpha, perhaps?"

"In the process of it, but no hard sightings yet."

"Even with Terros Sight... You're saying we have a clue, but we don't have a solid lead."

"Unfortunately. Same old struggle."

"Well, the Circle hasn't been a thorn in Trinity's side all these years for nothing." Cedar sighed. "I have to tell Gale." Hell, if it wasn't for Gale, it was unlikely Josh would have told her all of this. She might have heard the news in passing at one point, but this wasn't the sort of thing she typically needed to know to do her job.

"Do you think that's a good idea?" Josh asked.

"Probably not, but he needs to know. He deserves to know. I can't keep this from him. He can handle it."

At least, she hoped he could. She needed him to. Ike needed him to. It was time he picked his cub over chasing phantoms. If Gale left now, after all this progress, he really would be a lost cause.

CHAPTER 17

IT WAS GETTING LATE. Gale had called Mama Blanc when it was time for Ike to get out of school. She agreed to take care of him for a while, along with Papa Blanc. Gale said it was okay for them to explain the situation to him. Ike had a right to know, and Gale would talk to him more when they had all returned home. He had already cleared everything with Lance.

Lance was content allowing Gale to leave since Mateo was around. There was only one extra room, but Mateo and Austin would be staying in it—after the bed had at least been made presentable. Josh opted to sleep in the living room. They were able to clear just enough space in there to get a sleeping bag to fit on the floor.

Gale was ready to throw everything out because having anyone stay at the Lenkovs was a joke, but the others insisted this was fine. They had to tackle one issue at a time. And Lance wanted the witch to stay. He didn't say it outright, but he got irritable when Gale talked about having Josh stay with Weston and sending Mateo home with Austin for the night instead of bringing Austin here.

If Lance wanted to have his and Yuri's space invaded all night, he was very out of sorts.

"All good?" Gale asked.

"As good as it can be," Lance muttered. He brushed the dark hair away from his brother's forehead. The tiger shifter wasn't strung up so tightly now. The air wasn't thick with tension. It was easy to breathe.

"You might consider letting your tiger out and go for a quick run. You've been cooped up all day."

"My tiger is used to being neglected."

Mateo punched him in the arm. "That's not a good thing, you ass."

"Mateo," Austin said sternly.

"It's fine." Lance rubbed his arm. "How did such a nice and mellow guy end up with a crazy-ass wolf shifter, though?"

Mateo huffed. His eyes flickered yellow. "I need to

go for a run."

"Then do it."

"Come with me."

Lance shook his head. "I'm not leaving Yuri's side."

"I'll still be here," Austin offered. "I mean, if that makes you feel any better."

Lance studied the human quietly, almost like he was seeing him for the first time.

"Are you ogling my mate?" Mateo growled.

Lance rolled his eyes at the wolf. "Thanks, Austin. Maybe later."

"How about you, Josh. Are you good?" Gale asked.

"Yes. I have everything I need. Thank you, Gale."

"Is Cedar still outside?" She had made herself scarce after she and Josh went out for that *secret* talk earlier.

"Yes, she's waiting for you."

"I guess I better get going, then. If you guys need anything, just let me know."

"I definitely will," Austin replied. Gale felt better knowing Austin would be around. As a human, he wasn't as strong as a shifter, but he had a level head.

Gale left after that. Like he was told, Cedar was outside, leaning against the cabin, arms folded. She was staring at a specific point in the snow. Gale didn't see anything interesting. It looked the same as the rest of the blanketed white ground. He caught a scent, though. It was sour instead of the usual sweetness he had come to expect.

"Something wrong?" he asked.

"No," she said. "But I do have something I need to talk to you about. Later, after Ike is in bed."

"Does it have anything to do with what you and Josh talked about earlier?"

"Yes."

Gale didn't like the sound of that, but at least Cedar was being true to her word. She said she wouldn't hide anything from him again, so he agreed to be patient.

There was little talking on the way home. Gale would have preferred complete silence, but the snow made sure to punctuate each step they took with a dull crunch. It was like a fracture that was slowly growing into a deep cut, and it was between him and Cedar. He deluded himself into thinking he might get to keep her. But what if she was leaving? He couldn't find anything to say—though there was a lot he wished he could.

He was relieved when they made it to his cabin. Ike burst out the door, Mama and Papa Blanc behind him.

"How's Yuri?" the cub asked.

"He's doing okay. He's going to get better, Ike. We have someone who can help him," Gale said. And he smiled because it was a huge relief. After all this time, they'd be able to expel the unknown poison that had been slowly killing him all these years.

"No more seizures?"

"I don't know about that for sure, but he's going to get better." Gale turned to his parents. "Thanks for taking care of Ike."

Mama Blanc replied, "It's always a pleasure to spend time with my grandcub."

Ike gave his grandma and grandpa a big hug before seeing them off. Cedar was uncharacteristically quiet. She even physically removed herself from the exchange. She was always in the thick of things, but she took noticeable steps back here. It put Gale's polar bear on edge.

Goodbyes were kept brief, and against Ike's protests, it was time for him to go to bed. School would be out for a couple days, but it was best to keep this high-energy cub on a schedule. And Gale knew he was tired. He got extra wiry when he was exhausted.

Ike bounced on his bed like he intended to lift off. "Dad?"

"Yeah?" Gale caught him and wrestled him underneath his blanket.

"Can I see Yuri tomorrow?"

"Yes, you can. I'm sure Lance won't mind."

"Lance? Yuri's not awake?"

"Not when I left, but he might be awake tomorrow, just for you."

Ike glanced at Cedar, lingering in the doorway. "Dad?"

"Yeah, cub?" Gale grinned and tickled his chatty son.

Ike giggled and grabbed Gale's arms to stop his onslaught. Ike bit his lower lip, and his stormy gray eyes darted to the left. "Can I have a hug?"

It shouldn't have been a big deal. His cub shouldn't have had to ask. Gale's lips trembled as he quickly wrapped his arms around him. "Of course you can."

Ike hugged him back. "I love you."

"I love you, too. Do you know how proud you make me?"

"I make you proud?"

"Every day. You're growing up into a great polar bear."

"Do you think Mom would have been proud of me, too?"

"She's proud of your right now."

"Even though there's no aurora out?"

"Yep."

"Are you proud of me, Cedar?"

Cedar pushed off the door frame, walked over to Ike, kissed him on the cheek, and said, "I am. You're the best. Thanks for being my friend." She winked.

Ike lay down and pulled up his blanket so it was snug around his neck. "Good night."

"Good night," Gale and Cedar replied, leaving his room, turning off the light, and closing the door quietly behind them. They were silent in the cabin's short hall as they walked into the small square living room.

"Talk to me," Gale said. He didn't bother to sit on the couch. He couldn't bring himself to. "I can't wait anymore. Your scent is putting me on edge. What has you so scared?"

Cedar didn't say a word. She stepped up to him, real close, and then she placed her hands on his cheeks. Her big brown eyes shimmered as she experimented with holding his gaze. He held on to her wrists. Her pulse fluttered.

"Trinity thinks they've found a trail left by one of the Black Witches responsible for killing Iris's team."

Gale froze. He didn't know how to react. He had

to replay what she said over again in his head, and still he asked, "What?"

"Stay calm, Gale."

Why is she saying that? he wondered. How could she expect him to stay calm after hearing that? This was his mate she was talking about. He should leave. He could assist Trinity. He could kill those bastard witches for what they did.

"Gale." Cedar jerked back like he had burned her. She took his wrists and held his hands in front of his face. They were glowing white-hot. He was lighting up with explosive energy. It was getting brighter and brighter, so bright it hurt to look. His skin tingled. His bones ached. It was like his body was made up of a bunch of tiny sparks. He couldn't feel anything but the power.

Iris had told him about Solsis. He had seen her use it, but it never came to him. Until Cedar. Cedar arrived and suddenly Gale was exploding with Sun Magic. Why was that? What had changed? Was all of his progress a lie? A black hole in his chest nulled the static. His heart wasn't there. He couldn't feel it beating.

On the outside, he had been doing better. Even before Cedar, it looked like he was doing better, but his core was being eaten away by something almost as dark as the Black Magic killing Yuri.

Gale gritted his teeth, and the Solsis stayed. Hot. Hot. Hot.

"I can't do this anymore."

And there it was. He admitted it to himself. Something had to change. Something inside of him had to change. He had to end the anger and sadness or let it consume him once and for all.

"Remember everything I taught you," Cedar said. "Your son is in the other room. You don't want to hurt him."

How could he forget about that?

Just like that, he turned off the Sun Magic like all it took was a simple flip of a switch. The buzzing subsided, and his skin ceased to glow. But the agitation did not fade. The hole in his heart ached.

"I have to go," he said. He grabbed his coat, put on his boots, and opened the front door.

"Right now?" Cedar asked, following him into the snow. "When Christmas is less than a week away? You're going to leave your son after all the progress you've made on a 'maybe'? They don't know if they'll even be able to catch the witch—and they need to *catch* them. Killing them won't help anyone. We need answers to protect the future, Gale. This can't be about the past. It can't be about revenge. And you're not trained for this. You're not a peacekeeper."

"Trinity didn't help Mateo!" Gale roared. He kicked snow into the air as he came to a halt and spun around to face Cedar. "If I hadn't gone to Utah to save him when he ran off half-cocked, he would've been dead right now because of hunters *Trinity* chose to ignore. In all honesty, Cedar, I have no idea what to think of Trinity. The idea of a shifter alliance is appealing, but I don't *know* them, the ones in charge. I've trusted them and worked with them to whatever degree this is all because of my mate. I trusted *her*, and *she* trusted Trinity."

"Gale, nothing's perfect. I know Trinity can be hard to understand, but they are doing good things. More shifters are needed all the time, and maybe they didn't go after Mateo because they knew you would. They trust you. They know you do good things. You know they do good things too, whether you want to admit it or not. You're angry because Trinity couldn't save Iris, and I understand that, but Trinity is a better match for Black Witches than you are any day. You're not a warrior. Trinity has Sun Shifters who can use Solsis in ways you couldn't imagine. Me neither. I'm nothing compared to them. I've got a different role. So do you."

She reached out for him again, but he recoiled. A tear escaped one of her eyes, then the other, freezing on her skin. "Think about this, Gale. Really think about this."

He ran. The tingling was back, and his hands were lighting up. His whole body was lighting up. He was turning into Mateo, but even Mateo didn't have this kind of destructive power trapped inside of him. Gale hoped when he burst, he could go with it and cease to exist. He screamed into the darkness of night. "Iris!" He screamed so loudly, his vocal cords burned like they were being ripped to shreds.

And then someone was behind him, arms wrapped as far as they would go around his waist, a face buried into his lower back.

"Don't leave!" Ike begged. "Don't leave me, Daddy."

Gale could breathe again. The restriction in his chest, the buzzing energy, they receded for good. There weren't any residual sparks left behind.

"Please," Ike cried. "I'll do everything you want. I'll make you proud of me again. If I did something wrong, I'll fix it."

"You didn't do anything wrong." Gale took his

cub's hands and pried them off his waist so he could turn around and face him. He crouched down in the snow to meet his cub's watery eyes. "I won't leave you, Ike. Okay? I'm not leaving."

"Stay," Ike said. He wiped icy tears from his eyes and sniffled pitifully. He had no coat, no shoes. He was wearing his fuzzy pajamas. Gale took off his coat and wrapped it around his cub, then he lifted Ike into his arms to get his feet out of the snow.

"I'm staying," Gale said. "I'm sorry, Ike. I'm sorry for making you cry, for making you doubt me all the time. I'm not going to do it anymore." He looked up into the dark expanse of sky. "Iris, I'm not going to do this anymore." He shuddered and hugged Ike tighter. "I never apologized to you before, Ike. I never talked to you properly either. I know I show it terribly, and that I'm a bad dad, but you're everything to me. Everything. I love you more than anything, and yet I keep hurting you like this. I'll do better. I promise I will. I'm trying." Spirits, he was trying.

"You've been doing better. Especially with Cedar here." Ike offered a hesitant smile. "Keep doing that." He buried his face into his father's shoulder.

Cedar stood silently, wiping at her eyes. Gale moved Ike so he could hold him snugly in one arm and held out his other hand to her. She came forward and joined them in a group hug. It was the warmest hug Gale had shared in a long time. He had stopped feeling this kind of warmth because he was chasing after Iris, lost in his inability to bring her back or let her go. Lost in the unfairness of it all. But this was love, and it was time he opened up to it again. This could mend his heart.

He hadn't really been here for years. He was always searching for what he was supposed to do and lost in what he couldn't do.

No, Trinity didn't need him to hunt down the Black Witch, but they did need him in other ways. More importantly, he had a town full of shifters who depended on him in some capacity, even those who only stayed for a week or two. He was part of this town's foundation. A foundation needed to be stable. How could he do his best by all of these shifters if he was closed off to love? Maybe it was time to stop chasing shadows. Maybe he needed to put his family first.

CHAPTER 18

IT WAS CHRISTMAS DAY. The busy morning leaked into a busy evening, and Christmas dinner at the Lodge was a success. Cedar caught loads of prime fish. Gale and Ike did a lot of cooking and managed to get Cedar's approval—though she ended up delegating after being so adamant on them doing everything themselves before, not that Gale or Ike minded.

Toys littered the Lodge's floor in the dinner aftermath; it was cheerful madness. The kids were all having the time of their life. Since the town was so spread out and many residents didn't want electricity in their cabins, the Lodge was the only place they had bothered decorating. They invited all the residents, but Gale and

Weston insisted it be optional. Cedar had good intentions, and things were changing, but Eurio wasn't going to turn into a boot camp. And it was just as well. The Christmas turnout was excellent; almost eighty percent of Eurio was present. That was ten percent more than those who had attended the last Hunt. Cedar made sure Gale and Weston knew the numbers.

Gale had to admit that Cedar had outdone herself on the decorations. She had delegated that, too. The best feature was the large Christmas tree sitting in the center of the dining room. The angled roof left plenty of room for it to stand just over eleven feet tall. Getting it inside of the building had been a project, but it was worth it. It was decorated in layer upon layer of lights and shone like an aurora itself. It was more rainbow than Christmas, but it was a real hit with the kids. Austin did an art project with them at school where they each made their own ornament, giving the tree an even more personal touch.

Eurio's first Christmas was a success.

Gale sighed when he heard Lance swear. The tiger shifter was covered in the mashed potatoes and gravy he had just dished up. He wiped his eyes before the food could blind him and swore again. Yuri laughed at his side but quickly backed away when Lance swung his plate at him. He dropped the plate when he missed, and Gale silently thanked the spirits that it wasn't glass. Lance pounced on Yuri when he turned tail to run. Lance wrapped his arms tightly around his brother and rubbed his gravy-soaked cheek against his brother's, adequately sullying them both.

It was good to see Yuri was feeling like himself again.

After five days of treatment with Josh, he almost looked like a new tiger. The color in his skin was back to its natural rich tan tone. Those bruised circles under his eyes were nothing but a memory. He was smiling and charming as ever—or as obnoxious as ever; it depended on how he decided to use his magnetic personality. Before the seizure that caused his PWD, Yuri excelled at using words to amplify his natural charm.

A lot had changed in the time Gale had known the twins. He had witnessed their dynamics shift. Lance had always been dependent on Yuri. He had been happy to let Yuri lead, and he had been even more withdrawn inside of himself. But the seizure that caused Yuri's PWD left Lance scrambling. Suddenly, Yuri needed Lance in a way he never had. And since the two never let anyone else in, Lance took all of the responsibility upon himself. To be fair, Gale tried, but the two were just as strong-willed at sixteen as they were now at twenty-four.

Today, Lance was more at ease than Gale had seen him in a long time.

Gale picked at his food while others shoveled in mouthfuls. His appetite was better, but eating often felt like a chore. The same couldn't be said for Ike. The cub ate faster than almost anyone, and now he was running around with Neil. The two of them hadn't hit it off initially. It took Neil a while to warm up to everyone else in Eurio. It was typical behavior of wolves, especially those from naturalist packs. Trusting anyone outside of the pack was dangerous. Gale was glad to see he had loosened up and that Ike had been receptive. Neil's parents hadn't come to the Christmas celebration, but they allowed their son to, just like they allowed him to go to school. That was tremendous progress.

At last, Gale gave up on eating. He was full, so he had done well. It helped that the food tasted so good. He wrapped his arm around Cedar, who had finished well before him. She happily snuggled into him. Her head rested just under his chin, and he savored her warmth. He held her just a little tighter when he thought about how close he had been to leaving and ruining everything after hearing the news about the Black Witch Trinity was hoping to capture. He had thought it was his duty to avenge Iris. Now... now he was focused on Eurio. What Cedar had said struck a chord with him.

This was his role. Family was what he had always wanted. This was what he had always wished Iris had wanted. Maybe she had, but she hadn't wanted it the same way.

"Ike finally found the perfect wrestling buddy," Cedar said. "He doesn't completely overpower him like Mateo does."

"You're right about that," Gale said. "We'll see how long those new toys stay intact." Ike tossed an electronic car like it was an airplane as if to prove Gale's point. "Hey! You're supposed to drive it with a controller, not launch it!"

Cedar laughed.

"Sorry!" Ike ran to pick up the toy. Neil grabbed the controller. He pressed a button and the tires spun in Ike's grasp. He let out a startled yelp and the wolf shifter boy chortled. Ike handed him the car and scampered over to the grownups. He fixed his gaze on Cedar, not saying a word

"What's up, Ike?" Cedar asked and raised an eyebrow. "Why are you staring at me like that?"

"Are you going to stay here with us forever?"

"Do you want me to?"

"Yes!"

"I don't know," Cedar said with a smile. She was teasing. Gale hoped she was teasing.

Ike huffed and melted to his knees. He rested his chin on her lap and looked up at her with big gray eyes. "Please. You like it here, don't you? You like us, don't you?"

She ran her hands over the shaved sides of his head. "Yes, I like it here, and I like you."

"So, you'll stay?"

"You're a persistent little guy, aren't you?" She turned to Gale. "What do you think?"

"I think you should stay."

"Sounds like I'm staying, Ike."

"Thank you, Cedar." Ike jumped up onto his feet and gave her a big squeeze. Then he hugged Gale before running off again. He was likely heading back to Neil, but he wasn't watching where he was going and ran into Mateo. He almost knocked the much bigger shifter on the floor. Austin was safe on the sidelines, hand over his mouth, and eyes twinkling as he laughed.

"Boy bulldozer." Gale shook his head.

"That he is," Cedar agreed. But then she frowned. "What are we, Gale? Do you really want me to stay, too?"

"I'm offended you have to ask." He nibbled her ear and enjoyed the sight of goosebumps on her flesh. "But I've done plenty to make you doubt me. I'm sorry, Cedar. I'm sorry I almost left. I... asked for time before. I guess I thought with time I could become the perfect mate for you, but I'm not perfect. Nothing is. You said it yourself before. But I do know exactly where I'm needed now. I know what I can do. And I know what I want. I want to raise my cub and make up for lost time, and I want you to stay. Maybe I shouldn't, but I have to ask," he kissed her neck and felt the light rumble stemming from her chest, "will you do me the honor of becoming my mate?"

"The presents are never-ending," she said breathlessly. Then she turned, capturing his lips with hers.

"I'm not pressuring you into anything," he said. "But you should know how I feel. I don't want to leave any room for doubt. I mean it with all of my heart."

"I know you do." She kissed him again.

"You talked about how you weren't too keen on a mate before," he said. "I'm not pushing."

"Well, you don't expect me to become a baby factory, do you?"

"Of course not. One Ike is more than enough."

Cedar moved away from him, eyes wide. "Ike is a golden child."

"My point exactly. I'm not good enough for him."

Cedar's eyes softened. "You are, Gale. Maybe there's never a right time for anything. I'll never be Iris to you. It's not that I want to be, but I've fallen in love with you. I want to have something with you that belongs to just the two of us."

"We already do, Cedar. This, what we have between us, isn't about Iris at all."

She touched his cheek. "A selfish part of me wants you to forget her entirely, but I know that's not going to happen. I know you'll get sad sometimes and that you'll think of her. And you deserve to. She was a huge part of your life. But… when you're with me, please try to be *with* me."

Gale kissed her again, grabbed her thighs, and pulled her onto his lap so she was straddling him. "You have me."

"And," Cedar said against his lips, "you are a good kisser. I need kisses like this for the rest of my life. I'll stay here, and Trinity won't have to worry about Eurio slipping back to its old ways. Win-win."

Gale chuckled. "Now you're making this about work?"

"No way." She kissed him hard, sucked on his lower lip, and then pushed her tongue inside of his mouth. She tasted like cranberry sauce.

"You two do realize there are kids here right?"

The polar bears unlocked their lips to find a short shifter in a peacekeeper uniform standing in front of them with her arms folded.

"Ling!" Gale exclaimed. "When did you get here?"

"Just now," the peacekeeper said. She flicked her green-tinted brown eyes back and forth between the two polar bears before settling. "Hello, Cedar. I didn't know you two were a thing."

Cedar cleared her throat. "A lot changes in a month?"

"It's good to see you, Ling," Gale said.

"It's good to see you, too."

Gale wanted to smile, but he stopped short. Ling was a peacekeeper. She had worked closely with Iris in the past. She was also the panda bear who almost took Iris away from him and likely would have if Iris hadn't picked him in the end. Gale trusted Ling, though. He had a closeness with her he didn't have with anyone else and it was all because she had cared for Iris in the same way he did.

Part of him wanted to ask why she was her, but he was pretty sure he knew. And he knew he shouldn't ask. He needed to let it go. He needed to let Iris go.

"I'm sure Cedar told you about the Circle and the Black Witch trail we're on," Ling said.

Gale's face fell, but he didn't ask her to stop. He didn't have the strength to. The apparently masochistic side of him wanted to hear it.

"I'm sorry to report that the trail has gone cold. Again. We're doing our best to pick it back up, but the Circle somehow keeps giving us the slip. Every time we find something, it vanishes like smoke."

"I'm sorry, Gale," Cedar said as she rubbed his chest.

Gale grunted. "You'll get them eventually."

"I thought you should know. But that's not why I came." Ling fished inside one of the many pockets in her combat pants—Gale had never seen this woman without her peacekeeper gear—and pulled out a plain white envelope. "I found this letter." She held it out to Gale.

"What is it?" he asked.

"It's from Iris. I found it hidden in the room we

shared at Trinity HQ. I'm moving out, and the room is getting stripped apart. I never would have found the letter otherwise. It was underneath the floorboards. I only read the first line. It's for you."

Gale's hand trembled. He couldn't look at the envelope and pressed his hands into his thighs to keep them from trembling.

"You need some time alone?" Cedar asked.

"Later," he said gruffly.

"Now," Cedar countered. She kissed his cheek. "It's okay."

Gale was scared to look into her eyes, but he forced himself to. She didn't seem angry. Her brown eyes were soft and warm enough to make him melt.

"I'll watch Ike. If it gets too late and you haven't come back yet, we'll meet at your place."

"Our place," Gale corrected.

"Right. Our place." Cedar touched his cheek, gently running her thumb over the same place she had kissed him. "I won't make that mistake again. You can't forget either. I choose you and Ike."

Gale couldn't say no, then, to reading this letter and maybe putting this all behind him once and for all. Cedar would stay, and he believed her.

"Thanks." He gave her a quick hug, stood, and did

the same with Ling. Then he left the Lodge without another word. If he hadn't, they would have seen he
couldn't breathe.

Gale walked aimlessly in the snow, through the trees,
farther and farther away from Eurio; he was going as
far as he could. The goal was to be alone and in total
silence. He ended up following the Tanana River. It was
the steadfast guide that always oriented him when his
brain was spiraling. If he kept following the river, he'd
eventually end up in the next small town where he too
often drank himself senseless. The letter was in his
right hand. He gripped it just tight enough that he knew
it was still there. Iris's last words… He didn't know if
he would ever be ready to read them.

It was dark out, but not as dark as it could have
been. It was one of those special moments: an Aurora
was in the sky, phasing in and out and mirroring the
Tanana River itself; they held the same meandering
shape, too. Fish scales twinkled like stars in the water
and the snow was painted the same shades of blues and
greens as the aurora. Gale had grown up with this, but
tonight seemed bigger, grander.

Iris loved auroras. She would look up at one, and she would dream of the great big world out there. She'd look beyond the lights made up of the spirits and straight to the stars beyond. Gale had never looked beyond. He tried to find the eyes of the spirits watching him inside of the ribbon of lights.

"You have to stop walking sometime," he told himself.

His feet kept moving. Each time he flattened the snow underfoot, the sound grew a little louder, as if it were ricocheting off the nearby mountains. The parts of the river that weren't frozen produced a soft trickling sound that grew into a roar. Gale covered his ears and ended up sitting on a rock on the riverbank. He slouched and breathed deeply a few times before releasing his hands. He still held the envelope as his gloved hands touched the snow below. If he loosened his grip the slightest bit, the snow would claim the letter. He could leave it there and never read it—but that wasn't an option.

He lifted his hands. They trembled again, but he held fast. The blank envelope looked back at him, unassuming, wordless.

It could be anything.

He untucked the tongue, grabbed the paper inside,

and dropped the envelope in the snow. The paper was carefully folded in perfect thirds. It was plain and white aside from the words scrawled in black ink. No pink. No flower print. Iris had never been into that. She cared about function. In that way, she had fit Eurio perfectly.

Carefully, Gale unfolded the letter. He read the first two words: To Gale.

He read them again. To Gale.

He dropped his hands into his lap and puffed out his own little personal cloud. It dissipated to join the ether within seconds. He wondered if Iris was watching him now from the aurora. He wondered if those who had died stuck around. Then he thought of Ike and Cedar. He should have been with them, not here. It was Christmas night, and he was absent again.

"Let's get this over with," he said.

He forced his eyes back to the letter.

To Gale, my mate, and the love of my life.

I'm not sure why I'm writing this letter. A scenario where you'd have to read it instead of me talking to you face to face is not one I want to imagine. But the truth is this:

I'm a peacekeeper. Peacekeepers do danger-ous things, so this seems like a good idea. Worse than imagining me not being able to tell you this myself someday is you not ever hearing it at all because I never told you. Be-cause I don't know how to tell you.

Gale, you're the perfect mate. I could never have asked for anyone better than you. I know I don't show it very well, and I know I drive you crazy sometimes, but you still love me, and I love you. You and Ike are so im-portant to me, a big part of my world. I'm not very maternal by nature, so it's a good thing you're the family type. We complement each other in a way.

Always be yourself, Gale. You've tried to follow in my footsteps a time or two. That would be fine except it's never been what you wanted. You even talked about becoming a peacekeeper. I told you no, and I don't regret doing that. This isn't the kind of life you want. You like being rooted down, and I like flying free. I said we complement each other, but that's not entirely true. More often, we clash. And still you stay. I come back and it's like nothing has changed. You're mad at me for a moment, but then you forgive me.

I'm trying to say I realize I'm selfish.

But I am glad you're my mate, Gale. I'd be worried about Ike if he didn't have you. I can rest easy knowing that, while I'm away, you're with our cub. He adores you. He's only a year old, starting to say a few words, already determined to run around the entire town. He's a handful, but you're right there with him, and he needs that. He comes to you first. Make sure you're always like that for him Gale. Be the one he comes to first always. Root down like you're so good at and promise me that Ike will be okay no matter what happens in the future.

I'm sorry for every time I've hurt you. I'm sorry for every future time I'll hurt you too, because I know I will. That's what our relationship is. I don't know why you stay with me sometimes. Because I know. I know how much I hurt you. I don't know if you believe me when I say I love you because we love so differently. And because our priorities are not the same. Family doesn't come first for me, Gale. I have a different purpose. Fighting for the world, fighting for the freedom of many, for shifterkind, that's my priority. Staying in one place, being a good mother... that's not me. I was scared to death of having a cub, but I knew you wanted one. I thought I could give you something since I was so good at giving you nothing. When we lost our first, I had so many mixed feelings, and I'm not sure I could properly explain them now.

"I fucking know that," Gale said under his breath. He rubbed his eyes and held his fingers still against his temples. He wanted to put the letter away, but he had almost read it all. He just had to keep reading for a little longer. This was what he had been waiting for, wasn't it? Closure. He had been holding on to Iris for years, unable to let go. Maybe Iris knew him well enough to know this would happen if she died. That was why she wrote this letter. She did it for him.

If I die before I find a way to say all of this to you in person, read this letter and know that I want you to move on. I think you'll have a hard time with it. I think you'll use my memory to hold you back. I don't want to be your chains, Gale. I want to be

your wings. Find your path, and stop following me. I won't be there to chase anymore.

I love you. I love you so goddamn much.
My life has been immensely better because of
your love. Not many are lucky enough to
have a love like this, and it matters. I may be
flighty, I may have other priorities, I may be
restless and have a need to fight and defend,
but you made me better.

Thank you, my love.

Gale put the letter back down on his lap. He held
it in place with one hand as he wiped his leaking eyes
with the other. Every inch of him hurt. Solsis wasn't
rising to the surface in response this time, though.
There was no buzzing energy or anger. He was aware
of the black hole in his heart, but it was different. It
wasn't so wide or so deep. It was mending, sealing over
with new love, with the change in himself to let that
new love in. He could say goodbye now. He could finally do it.

"I love you, Iris. Always will."

He stood from his rock and walked close to the icy
edge of the river. He crumpled up the letter into a ball

and tossed it into a section where the water wasn't frozen over. He let the Tanana River take her away. He let it free her as she merged into the aurora and sprouted wings. Then he left. He was going back to Eurio, to his family. He was going back to Ike and Cedar.

CHAPTER 19

"WILL DAD COME HOME soon?" Ike asked.

Cedar replied, "He'll be back before you wake up tomorrow."

The cub's eyes were heavy. He wouldn't be awake much longer. Christmas Day had been busy in the best way. The only thing that didn't make it perfect was that letter from Iris. But Cedar was doing her best not to be selfish. Gale probably needed that letter more than anything else this Christmas. Maybe. She didn't know. She just knew she had to be here for him.

"Okay." Ike yawned. When he blinked his eyes, they almost didn't open again. "Good night, Cedar."

"Good night, Ike."

Cedar snuck out of his room. Ike had said he didn't need to be tucked in, but he did like the attention. And the kid could be a real chatterbox when he was in the mood. He told her Gale didn't often tuck him in, but if he was with his grandparents, they tucked him in without fail.

Cedar sighed against the closed wooden door and listened to the quiet house. The lights were off so there was no buzzing electricity. The house was well insulated, and they were polar bears, so there was no humming heater at the moment either. She debated on if she should head to her own room for the night or wait up for Gale. Then the front door opened, making the decision for her.

Gale was here. His eyes were puffy and red. He looked tired, and he was empty-handed. He could walk in a straight line though, so he wasn't drunk. Cedar stepped forward to meet him. He wrapped his arms around her, held her close, and bent down to bury his face in her shoulder. He didn't smell like cheap booze, so he hadn't been drinking at all. She hugged him back.

"You okay?" she asked.

"Yeah. Because you're still here."

"I told you I would be."

"I know. I'm just… I'm just glad."

Cedar held him tighter. "I want to stay."

"Where would Ike end up without you setting me straight?"

"You were already working your way back without me. Hell, things aren't perfect now or anything, but they're different."

"You say that like destiny didn't plan on sending you here for me and Ike."

"You believe in destiny, Gale?"

He shrugged, stood upright, and looked down at her. He caught her eye and said, "Probably. I don't know how else this would have happened."

Cedar shrugged. "Sometimes life just works out that way. Random chance."

"You can believe in random chance, and I'll believe in destiny." He cracked a smile.

"Fine." Cedar smiled back. "What did Iris say?"

"Exactly what I needed to hear. Guess she had some foresight and knew me better than I thought she did."

"Did you keep it?"

"Would you be upset if I had?"

Cedar shook her head. "Of course not. I was just curious."

"I didn't. I gave it to the river."

"Does this mean you're ready to make me your mate?" Cedar unzipped his coat and tapped his chest.

"Are *you* ready?" he countered. "You don't think it's too fast? You're not going to regret it?"

"We've been spending a ton of time together. I think I know your heart by now, Gale. Our first time... wasn't the best, but it was kind of my fault, too. Trinity warned me about you."

Gale snorted. "Did they?"

"Yeah, they wanted me to become your therapist."

"Really?" He raised an eyebrow.

"Okay, no, they didn't say that. But it was kind of implied. They just wanted me to make sure you were well enough to take care of Eurio alongside Weston."

"Fair enough."

"I wasn't expecting you to be so sexy, though."

Gale rolled his eyes. "You were just as wet for that grizzly you arrived with."

"Hey! He was pretty fine too," she traced his lips with her finger, "but not like you. Somehow, I think you're even sexier than you were when I first laid eyes on you. I've never fallen in love with someone before. It's different than attraction. You were trying to tell me that when we talked about mates. Now I know why someone would want one." She grabbed the back of his neck and urged him to bend down. He did, and they kissed. She kissed him over and over, relishing the contented, low rumbles he made. "Are you ready now?" Cedar whispered.

"Very ready," Gale growled. He held her tighter, kissed her neck. "Stay with me, Cedar. I'll adore you all of my life, and I'll do my best not to fuck up."

"Me too." She put some space between them so she could flatten her hand against his heart. The beat was steady, but it fluttered at her touch. Anticipation. Excitement. She could smell it on him. His arousal was addicting, and her body reacted in kind. "Make love to me."

Gale kissed her again. Cedar tried to stay rooted in place, to kiss him back fiercely, but Gale wanted to move. He walked forward, forcing her to walk backward and to rely on his guidance so she wouldn't run into anything. He reached around her, pressing his arm into her waist, and opened the door. They were in his bedroom. He flicked on the light, shut the door, and locked it. Cedar made a grab for his coat and gloves. He was wearing way too many layers. It would be better if he was wearing, well, nothing.

He helped her out by shedding his clothes quickly.

Then he went for her sweater, pulled it over her head, undid her bra, and took off her pants. He acted like he couldn't get rid of them fast enough; it was a whirlwind of fabric as he discarded all of it onto a pile on the floor with his clothes. Then he grabbed her plump ass. She let out an exaggerated moan, lost in how he could command her body with a touch. She was wet as wet. Her arousal dripped down her inner thighs. Her pussy throbbed. Her legs shook. This wasn't like before when she and Gale had had sex. It was so much more. Her heart threatened to burst right out of her chest.

Cedar traced Gale's happy-trail with light fingers. She liked the way his stomach lurched under her touch and the shortness of breath that followed. She was making him wild. She grabbed his thick cock, admiring how hard he was for her already. She ran her hands down his shaft and gingerly touched the swollen red head dripping with precum.

Gale groaned and took her hands away. "That gets me way too fucking excited," he said. "Get on the bed. I want to eat you out."

"Okay," Cedar said easily. She was more than willing to experience that again, the ecstasy of his lips on her sensitive flesh... She got goosebumps just thinking about it. She skipped over to his bed and watched as

Gale eyed her breasts, her thighs, every exaggerated movement. Then she sat down, propped up some pillows behind her, and spread her legs wide for him. She was more than happy to show him everything. No one made her body feel as good as her soon-to-be mate did.

She giggled and exclaimed, "You're going to be my mate!" She covered her mouth right after, realizing it sounded stupid, like she was a teenage girl again. But it was a big deal for her. And she was ready for it. She was ready for him. Because if anyone was going to stand by her for the rest of her life, it was him.

Gale chuckled. "You're cute. Apparently, you liked some of what I did to you last time."

Cedar's body trembled as he stalked forward like a predator. "I've never had a guy eat me out before. I definitely liked it."

"That is a crime." Gale got on the bed, forced his way in between her legs, and kissed her lips. "But I'm glad that it was me. And it's only going to be me."

"Yes," Cedar agreed. "Just, yes."

"Lie down, beautiful."

Cedar did as she was told, and Gale followed her down. He kissed all over her face, down her neck, to her collarbones, where he introduced his teeth as he gently nibbled her skin. He kept as close as possible as he doted on her, and Cedar savored the feel of his skin on hers. Warmth. Comfort. Safety. Gale was all of those things. He palmed her large breasts, kneading and molding them at the same time. He swirled his thumbs around her nipples, making sure they were good and hard. Then he picked one to suck. His teeth grazed her sensitive skin, and she arched her back upward. Her breathing became shallow.

"Your boobs are fantastic," he said.

"They are quite nice," she managed to reply. "I'm proud of them."

Gale chuckled again. "I love you, Cedar. Stay with me."

"I'm with you. I love you too, Gale. I do. I'm staying." She ran her fingers through his brown hair and thought about how badly he had needed a haircut when she first met him. He was nicely groomed now. She took credit for that, thank you very much.

Gale worked farther down her body, kissing her stomach and getting dangerously close to her sex before he skipped it and moved straight to her thighs. He was ratcheting up the tension on purpose. But she held fast, determined to enjoy every second of this. She wondered if this was a test, if he was trying to get her to beg. *Well, challenge accepted,* she thought. She stayed as quiet as she could as she watched him, felt him. He greedily licked the moisture running down her thighs like she was life's sweet nectar itself. Her pussy throbbed, begging for his lips and tongue.

"Gale, please," she said, giving in. She couldn't take it anymore.

He looked up at her with a lazy smirk. He *was* waiting for her to beg. He kissed up her thigh and dove in between her legs. Cedar's eyes fluttered as Gale held her thighs and pushed forward, lips against her wet folds. Goosebumps rose all over her body. Then he licked her. She whimpered. She did her best not to get too loud so she wouldn't disturb Ike, but her whole body trembled. He licked her again. She gritted her teeth and made a grab for his wavy hair. She was already on the verge of coming. All he had to do was flick his tongue against her clit, nibble with his teeth, and her pussy was throbbing. She came hard.

He didn't give her a moment to calm down either. Her clit was so sensitive that when he licked it again, she nearly died. Then he thrust his fingers inside of her quickly, three at once, not waiting for her to adjust. The pain was almost blinding. Her vision went white for an instant as he rode out her waves of pleasure around his fingers. She came again. He was so damn good at this it was unbelievable.

By the time he was done, Cedar was breathing hard, collapsed on the bed. She hadn't screamed—which she was pretty sure she deserved a medal for. Then again, she was much too tired. Her hands weren't even in Gale's hair anymore. She had no control like this. When he licked her sensitive clit again, she said, "God. Stick it in me already. I think you're going to kill me if you keep this up."

"No way, but you might pass out from the pleasure," he replied.

"You gonna stick it in me?"

"Condom?"

"No condom. All of you, Gale. I'm back on the pill since our last tumble, and I'm not so averse to cubs anymore anyway."

"I thought the pill didn't agree with you."

"Eh, it's fine. It just wasn't worth it when I wasn't having sex with anyone anyway." She was touched he remembered her saying that, though.

"All right." Gale grabbed her thigh and angled her hips so he could slap her ass. She yelped, but the sting got her throbbing again.

"But that doesn't mean I'm in a hurry," she said breathlessly. "For cubs."

"I understand. I'm not either, to be honest. But if we ever change our minds, Ike would love a sibling." Gale kissed her stomach. "I have my New Year's resolution already."

"Oh?"

"Best dad of the year."

"Good resolution."

After making sure Cedar was positioned how he wanted, feet pressing into the bed and knees up, Gale snuggled himself in between her legs and on top of her. Cedar closed her eyes for a moment to simply take in the feeling of his skin on hers. She ran her hands down his sides, feeling his toned muscles, his heat. Then he bucked his hips, hitting her just right. Cedar moaned, but his lips were on hers, and he swallowed it. He gave another hard thrust and buried himself as far as he could inside of her with that one motion. Cedar's eyes rolled back in a mixture of pain and pleasure. She was very ready for him, so lubrication wasn't an issue, but his size was a lot to take. He gave her a couple seconds to adjust to it. She huffed out a breath, but she didn't want to wait.

She said, "Move."

He did.

Gale moved fast, hard, and relentlessly. The

twinge of pain inside of Cedar quickly faded away in place of pure ecstasy. She moaned and whimpered his name over and over, continuing to do her best to keep it down. A possessive snarl took Gale's lips, and Cedar knew he was going to mark her, rip into her skin so any other bear who might see her would know she was taken this breeding season—except it wasn't breeding season. This was different. It was for always. And then he did it, between her neck and right shoulder. His teeth clamped down on her flesh, and they sunk in deep, drawing hot blood. He thrust and thrust, and energy burst inside of Cedar again as she came. With Gale, she had learned that not all orgasms were equal. This one would have done her in if she hadn't been set on what she would do next.

She growled, pushed at his chest, and Gale got the message. He rolled them over so she was on top of him. She somehow drove through her exhausted body, rode her continuous orgasm, and rolled her hips against him fervently. It was Gale's turn to look helpless. She felt her teeth grow sharp, her own desire to make her lover submit. She bit his chest and sank her teeth into his right pec. He lost it. He shouted her name. He shouted, "Cedar!" And he spilled everything inside of her, wave after wave. There was too much for her to hold. The hot liquid dripped down her inner thighs, coating both of them in the aftermath of their coupling.

They were sweating, breathing heavily, still connected, but finally their frantic movements had slowed. Then they came to a stop.

Cedar brushed her long hair back and licked the bite on Gale's chest, wiping away the blood. He pushed himself up with one hand behind him, holding her with the other, as he did the same to the bite he had given her. It felt so good. The bites were deep and would scar. Neither of them was pulling any punches. The pain was the farthest thing from Cedar's mind, though. There were too many endorphins coursing through her body for her to care.

"I have a mate," she said. She shook her head and smiled. Then she kissed Gale on the lips. He kissed her back, the saliva, their blood, the taste of everything that was them, mingled together.

"Yes, you do. I'm yours, Cedar."

She rolled her hips against him one more time just to see him pant underneath her, and then she slowly moved away, disconnecting them. He was spent at the moment, and it felt good to know that she had done that to him. She lay down beside him, cuddling, and he wrapped his arm around her again.

"This is the best Christmas present I've ever had," she said. "All of this. Being able to call you and Ike my family."

"There's nothing more important than family," Gale said.

"I know, and yet I'm such a hypocrite. All this time I lectured you about being there for Ike, but it's been a long time since I've seen my own family. You'll have to come with me to meet them, or I'll have to find a way to convince them to visit Eurio."

"Either way," Gale agreed.

"I'm never going to lose sight of this again."

"Family?"

"Yeah."

"Me neither."

Gale kissed her sweetly. This was what she had been searching for ever since she left the Ruet Clan: her place in the world. It was all here in Eurio. And she was happy to root down if it meant keeping this always. Nothing out there could be better than this for her. She had to see the world first, set out on her own before she realized it, and that was okay too. Because she was home.

EPILOGUE

EVEN THOUGH CEDAR HAD stayed up late at the Lodge with everyone else for New Year's Eve last night, she was awake bright and early—or not so bright as was the case this time of year in Alaska. She had too much energy. And she was caffeinated way beyond what she probably should've been. Instead of alcohol, everyone resorted to caffeine to see how long they could stay up. Some of them even stayed up all the way through the night and into the morning, so Cedar wasn't the only one awake. But most everyone had crashed in the Lodge like this was some big slumber party. Yuri was there, too. He was doing much better, little bit by little bit. His PWD was still very much intact, but his eyes contained a bright light. He had energy again and was showing some of his true colors. He was a tease and a troublemaker as far as Cedar could tell. But the important thing was this: whatever Josh was doing was working.

Cedar went to the kitchen to get herself some water. She was craving more caffeine but figured it was probably best not to go there. The water rushing from the sink seemed louder than usual since the Lodge was so quiet. She nearly had a heart attack when she turned to see Weston in the doorway.

"Warn a girl." She growled and narrowly caught her cup from hitting the ground.

"You had way too much caffeine."

"Probably, but at least I stayed up until midnight. You left early with your mate."

"I take sleep when I can get it. Getting old and tired."

"You're only forty-four."

Weston shrugged. "Looks like last night was a hit, though. It's a fucking mess in there." Weston tilted his head back toward the dining room, pointing with his nose.

"You could say that," Cedar replied. She stared at

the ceiling and leaned back against the counter. "How long ago did I send my letter?"

"A few weeks for the first, about a week for the second," Weston said. "But I had to send both off with one of our Trinity contacts in Fairbanks since your clan doesn't live in the most accessible place. Delays are expected."

Cedar sighed. "I know. They live out in the middle of nowhere. I'm lucky there was anyone willing to deliver the letters at all."

"Indeed."

Cary popped her head into the kitchen. "Bruiser's here."

"What? Why?" Cedar asked.

Bruiser walked into the kitchen, holding out a letter. "That's the thanks I get for bringing this to you?"

Cedar accepted the letter and looked up at the bear with a bad eye. "Is this what I think it is?"

"A reply from your parents. Since you sent another letter before we got a chance to send the first one, they replied to both."

"Great!" Cedar tore into the letter. She scanned its contents quickly and was relieved to find her family was willing to come down to Eurio and stay for a while. They wanted to see where she lived, wanted to meet her mate and his cub, and they missed her. Tears burned her eyes, and she sniffled.

"Bad?" Bruiser asked.

"Not at all." Cedar wiped her eyes. "Mr. Nosy."

"I was in the area, so I thought I'd bring this to you while checking how things are going."

"I thought Ling was in charge of regular check-ins with Eurio again. You know, since I'm here to keep an eye on Gale."

"That would have been true if the situation wasn't what it currently is." Bruiser smirked. "Here you are, mated to the very bear Trinity's been worried about. You work fast, woman."

"Hey, I didn't come here planning on finding a mate."

"Your scent told me otherwise."

Weston cleared his throat. "Too much information." But Cedar could tell he was teasing by the light tone in his voice.

"It just turned out like this," Cedar said. "Gale called it destiny."

Bruiser nodded. "I hope you're happy, then."

"I am. Thanks, Bruiser. Anyway, back to work. I can take you back to my files and give you a tour of the place to inspect the changes I've helped implement. I've got digital and hard files you can take back with you if you want. Everything in them is up to date now."

"Good girl."

The kitchen was becoming the place to hang out because Gale and Ike barged in too.

"What are you doing?" Ike demanded. "Are you having fun without us?" He ran up to Cedar and grabbed her arm, swinging back and forth.

"Way too much energy going around for you last night," Cedar said. "You even stayed up practically all night. How can kids do that without caffeine?"

"I'm not tired!" he exclaimed. "It's hard to sleep when there's a lot going on."

"You'll crash tonight. You'll sleep for ten hours at a time if I let you."

Gale chuckled. "He has to make up for expending all of this energy somehow." Then he marched forward and stole a kiss from Cedar. He meant to be quick, but Cedar pulled him in for a longer one.

"How's it going, Gale?" Bruiser asked like he was oblivious to the two of them making out.

Gale cocked his head. "Bruiser, I didn't even realize you were here."

"Clearly. You're too involved in your mate."

"There is never 'too involved in your mate,'" Cedar

countered.

"Once I've checked and okayed everything, Ling will be doing regular check-ins again."

"You should stay a while, Bruiser," Cedar said. "Take a break."

"No."

"You won't regret it! I'll challenge you to a fishing competition."

Gale rolled his eyes. "Try it if you want. She'll tan your hide."

Cedar grinned.

"Maybe next time. I'm on a schedule," Bruiser said.

Cedar bumped his arm with her elbow. "Live a little. Trinity won't mind if you take the day to play."

Bruiser reiterated, "A *tight* schedule."

"All right, but it's your loss." Cedar took Gale's hand and squeezed it. "Eurio is a magical place. If you stayed a while, I think you'd see that, too. I had no idea I needed saving when I got here, but Eurio saved me. Its shifters did. And there's always room to grow in this family."

"I'm glad you feel that way because, if you pass my inspection, there are some shifters Trinity wants to send your way. We really don't have room anywhere else right now."

"Eurio's open to anyone," Weston said.

"Then let's get down to it."

Get Lance and Yuri's story in *Valentine's Day Tigers*.

BOOKS BY KESTRA PINGREE

Marked by the Moon
Her True Wolf
Her Brave Wolf
Her Fierce Wolf
Her Wild Wolf
Her Noble Owl
Her Bad Cat

The Lost Princess of Howling Sky
Phantom Fangs
Taken by Werewolves
Saving the Werewolves
Queen of Werewolves

The Holiday Shifter Mates
Halloween Werewolf
Christmas Polar Bear
Valentine's Day Tigers

These Immortal Vows
Demon Snare
Angel Asylum
Desire

Guardian

On the Precipice

The Soul Seer Saga

The Wandering Empath

The Lonely King

The Lost Souls

The Beautifully Cursed

The Lunar Dancer

Novels

Blind to Love

NEWSLETTER

Never miss a new release by signing up for Kestra's newsletter.

kestrapingree.com/subscribe

MESSAGE FROM THE AUTHOR

Thank you for reading *Christmas Polar Bear*.

If you enjoyed the ride, please consider leaving a review. Tell your friends too. If you're anything like me, you're already shouting your favorite stories from the rooftops. I commend you.

Your support is what allows me, and so many wonderful authors, to write these stories for you, so thank you.

From the bottom of my heart, thank you.

ABOUT THE AUTHOR

Kestra Pingree is a creative who doesn't know how to stop. They are first and foremost a writer and storyteller with an endless library of books in their head just waiting to be typed. They are also an artist and animator, as well as a singer, songwriter, and voice actor. One day they swear they're going to make their own video game, too.

If it involves creating, they are there.

They can also be seen cuddling their cat, reading, or playing video games.

kestrapingree.com

CPSIA information can be obtained
at www.ICGtesting.com
Printed in the USA
LVHW090804210620
658607LV00002B/224

9 781078 738859